**She'd anticipated kissing his full lips from the moment he picked her up. She already knew that when their lips touched, it would be divinely explosive.**

She watched him with anxious anticipation as he walked around the car to her passenger door. Opening it, he held out his hand. She took it, and her pulse quickened. Serenity wondered if he would

he

sex

her

for

cau

emb                   aware of her femininity cradled by his frame. She liked it there.

"Oops."

"I've got you." Chris's voice lowered. The husky tone was drowned in seduction.

For a moment neither of them moved. Chris wrapped his arms around her body. She could have lived right there.

"Mmm," she moaned, nestling against him.

Serenity closed her eyes for a moment. She felt Chris's hands run through her hair. She moaned again. With her head nestled in his chest, she could feel his heart rate quicken.

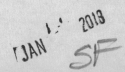

Dear Reader,

I'm so excited for you to take this journey into the lives of Serenity Williams and Christian Chandler. I wanted to take a very modern concept like online dating and explore the possibilities of a happily-ever-after, but with a little twist.

At first, Serenity and Christian are both opposed to the idea of finding love online. Serenity's friend actually creates a profile for her on a popular dating app as an attempt to get Serenity back into the dating game. For Christian, it's a different story. He simply wants to see what is out there and isn't taking it seriously at all. In fact, he uses a fictitious name because the last thing he expects to do is find love.

To both of their surprise, they find each other, and the magnetism between them is impossible to deny. Christian is falling for Serenity faster than he'd ever imagined, and knows he has to tell her the truth soon. He plans to do just that, but one explosive night and an unexpected emergency get in the way. Now that the stakes have risen, he has to find a way to tell the truth and risk losing her all at the same time.

I hope you enjoy the journey as Christian finds his way back to Serenity's heart. It is indeed a lovely journey that will take you halfway around the world.

Ciao,

*Nicki*

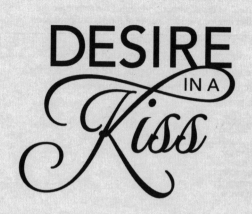

# DESIRE IN A Kiss

# NICKI NIGHT

HARLEQUIN® KIMANI™ ROMANCE

Recycling programs
for this product may
not exist in your area.

ISBN-13: 978-0-373-86528-4

Desire in a Kiss

**HARLEQUIN®**
www.Harlequin.com

**Printed in U.S.A.**

**Nicki Night** is an edgy hopeless romantic who enjoys creating stories of love and new possibilities. Nicki has a penchant for adventure and is currently working on penning her next romantic escapade. Nicki resides in the city dreams are made of, but occasionally travels to her treasured seaside hideaway to write in seclusion. She enjoys hearing from readers and can be contacted on Facebook, through her website at nickinight.com or via email at NickiNightwrites@gmail.com.

## Books by Nicki Night

### Harlequin Kimani Romance

*Her Chance at Love*
*His Love Lesson*
*Riding into Love*
*It Started in Paradise*
*Desire in a Kiss*

This book is dedicated to my hero, who inspires me to share love with the world. I love you, Les Flagler.

## Acknowledgments

As always, I must first thank the one who makes it all possible, my savior, my father, my comforter, God!

I can't thank my editors and team over at Harlequin Kimani enough. Your guidance and patience are unmatched. Thank you, Glenda Howard and Keyla Hernandez.

To my calm, cool and collected agent, Sara Camilli, thanks for being my advocate.

To my sisters in the craft, Beverly Jenkins, Brenda Jackson, Zuri Day, Donna Hill, Tiffany L. Warren, Yahrah St. John, Sheryl Lister, Elle Wright, Sherrell Green, Angela Seals, Iris Boling and so many others. Thanks for being my mentors, partners, sisters and inspiration.

To my family, I adore you and am so grateful for your willingness to share me with my passion. I love you Les, Lil Les, Milan and Laila. To Shawana Kenner and Shannon Harper, thanks for indulging my contests and coming up with great names for my heroes.

To my street team, readers, book clubs and book lovers, I couldn't be me without you. I'm eternally grateful! Keep reading and I'll keep writing!

To all book publishing allies, editors, promoters, bloggers, booksellers and librarians, thank you, thank you, thank you! I can't say it enough.

# Chapter 1

Serenity Williams looked up at the man across from her in the swanky restaurant. His mouth moved as furiously as his animated gestures. A smile. Hearty laughter. A wink. Hands tossed in the air. Serenity forced a half-cocked smile. It was the most she could manage having no idea what he'd just said. She'd zoned him out several minutes before, hearing the voice but no longer making out his words. His voice droned on. She was sure he was still talking about himself. Had he even asked about her? They had to have been at the table for at least an hour.

Entertaining herself, Serenity allowed her thoughts to wander from her crazy work schedule to creating ministories about the people her eyes landed on in the restaurant. Still, she maintained some level of consistent eye contact with her rambling date. The shifts in his motions clued her in on when to tilt her head sideways to appear engaged or spread her lips into an attentive-looking grin.

Serenity felt cynical, a feeling that didn't sit with her well. She loved people. Never had she been so uninterested in what a person had to say. But this man in front of her, the self-absorbed Mark Stapleton, had trampled on her attention span and hadn't bothered to notice when she disengaged.

A lanky waiter with long blond hair pulled back into a low ponytail came to remove their plates. Her meal was only slightly touched. Serenity welcomed the interruption, smiling at the waiter as if she were happy to see him. Mark stopped talking long enough to allow the space for the young man to ask if she would like to take her meal home.

"And the check, please." Mark dismissed the man's presence and went right back to speaking highly of himself. He paused again to take a sip of wine. Placing the glass on the table, he sighed and grinned, seemingly impressed with himself. "There's a nice lounge down the street," he said matter-of-factly.

"Huh? Oh…uh…" Serenity shook her head, then smiled apologetically. "Sorry. I have to be up really early tomorrow to work with some of my kids. Maybe another time?"

"You have children?" Mark reared his head back.

"No. I'm referring to the kids I give music lessons to."

"Oh!" He looked relieved.

Another turnoff.

The waiter returned with her carryout package and the check. Serenity was thankful the date was finally coming to an end.

Mark stood, extending to his full six feet of handsome tautness, and waited for her to get up from the table too. Strong features etched his face perfectly, drawing sharp lines in his jaw. Broad shoulders and a slim waist impeccably filled a well-fitting suit. He was undoubtedly attractive. Serenity also wouldn't deny that his résumé was impressive. A proud engineer. A fraternity man. There was enough to admire about Mark, but Serenity was the type to regard others as much as she did herself, and he simply didn't. They'd shared a meal, and he knew nothing about her. She wasn't an attention-seeker, but she didn't enjoy feeling discarded.

"Thank you for a wonderful meal." Serenity was being honest. The food was delicious, despite the fact that she'd lost her appetite shortly after it arrived.

"I'll just come by your place." Mark closed the space between them and ran the back of his finger down her cheek.

Serenity's skin tightened there. "Oh…I think it's a little too soon for that."

"Oh, you're one of *those*." Mark stepped back, pulled on his suit jacket and held his hand out, indicating that she should lead the way.

Serenity bit back a snide remark and headed toward the door. Mark saw her to her car, a practical crossover, filled with instruments and other items for the kids she taught. At first glance, it looked like the vehicle of a soccer mom.

"Thanks again, Mark." She nodded politely, slipping into cordial professionalism as if she were at the end of a business meeting instead of a date.

"Good night." He leaned forward, folding himself lower to meet her lips.

Curiosity led Serenity to let it happen. No spark. That sealed it for her. A second date wouldn't be necessary.

Confidently, Mark said, "Call you tomorrow," as if he'd be doing her a favor. He slid his thumb across her cheek, winked and opened her door. At least he had some gentlemanly qualities.

Mark was still standing beside her car after she'd closed her door, so she rolled down the window. He leaned into the opening. "Listen, we're adults…" She thought she saw him lick his lips. "Why deny ourselves? It's obvious that I like you and you like me." Serenity resisted the urge to roll her eyes at the confident jut of his chin as he spoke. "How about I come with you? We'll have another drink or two, and I'll show you what a great lover I can be."

Serenity cut her eyes, rolled up the window and jabbed the keys into the ignition. Mark jumped back when she revved the engine. The tires screeched as she jammed the car into Reverse and pulled off. Halfway down the block, she called her best friend, business partner and coworker, Rayne Alexander, through the car's Bluetooth system.

"It's over already?" Rayne's voice boomed.

"No more matchmaking. Promise me!" Serenity pointed as if Rayne were right in front of her.

"Ha!" Rayne's laugh was boisterous. "That bad, huh?"

"Yes!" Serenity said, rolling her eyes.

"De-*tails*!"

"Mark Stapleton is quite fond of Mark Stapleton. This arrogant man invited himself to my house so he could show me what a great lover he could be. I've known him for what—" she looked at the clock on the dashboard "—three hours. Ugh!"

"No!"

"Oh, yes!"

"What did you say?"

"I let my *tires* do the talking."

"What a pig!"

"Great minds…" Serenity realized she was speeding. Both her driving and her heart rate were accelerated. "And his love for himself is unnatural. In that short amount of time, I already know which name brands fit him best. He drives a Range Rover that he bought all-cash. He's the best engineer his company has seen in decades. His employers didn't actually say it, but that's what he believes and felt compelled to share with me. That man's arrogance is off the charts. When I told him I had to go home because of early appointments, he was clearly annoyed. You should have seen his face twist when he thought I had kids. Let's just say we're *not* compatible."

"Shame! He's so damn good-looking!"

"I won't deny that. But I need more than a gorgeous face. How about a man that I can actually hold a conversation with, one who's willing to hear what I have to say and doesn't expect me to have sex with him on the first date? I have a feeling that if I had met Mark before I lost all the weight, he wouldn't have given me a first look."

"You were beautiful then, and you're beautiful now."

"Of course," she said, chuckling.

Several moments of silence passed between them.

"Are you upset that it didn't work out?"

Serenity could detect the caution in Rayne's question. "Nah." She waved off Rayne's concern virtually. "You know my schedule is nuts. I'm trying to spend any extra time I have working off these last ten pounds." Serenity threw her head back and grunted. "These suckers are clinging to me like a leech."

Serenity talked with Rayne until she reached home. Their conversation turned from Mark to weekend plans to Rayne's upcoming engagement party.

"Hey!" Serenity perked up at Rayne's sudden excitement. "I could introduce you to one of Ethan's friends at the party."

"Rayne, no!" Serenity laughed as she pulled into her apartment complex. "Conversation over, lady. I'll talk to you tomorrow." Serenity cut off Rayne's snicker by ending the call.

Rolling to a stop in her designated parking spot, Serenity shut the ignition off and flopped against the back of her seat. Reflecting on the horrible date, she thought about what characteristics she'd actually like in a man. She didn't mind confidence and ambition. In fact, she found those traits rather attractive, but intelligence combined with a little humility and compassion made for a winning combination. She didn't require a male supermodel. More important than anything was honesty. After uncovering a few lies her ex-boyfriend, Jason Ruffin, had told, which he had labeled as *misunderstandings*, she felt compelled to add that to the list of must-haves in a relationship.

Casting those thoughts aside, Serenity climbed out of the car and made her way to her apartment. Closing the door behind her, she looked around, treasuring the coziness of her space. The decor was personal, reflecting the things she loved—music, art and kids. The living room had an energetic feel, with instruments propped on floating shelves, mix-matched yet eclectic furnishings stylishly pulled together. Every item held significance. Warmth radiated there.

She'd been alone for a while now—a little over a year. Not lonely, just alone. For the first time in a long while, she wondered what it would be like to carve out space in her life for a man.

# Chapter 2

Christian Chandler sailed through The Reserve wine bar and headed toward the back offices, taking in the tempo of the jazz music that flowed through the sound system. Inside his office, he tossed his car keys on the desk, one of three in the rectangular room. The other belonged to his partners, Kent Adams and Raymond Gray. Chris looked at his watch. Kent would be walking in any moment, but Ray would be late as usual.

Picking up a pile of mail, Chris sorted through it absentmindedly, as the music faded into the background. Last night's date moved to the forefront of his thoughts. He wished it had gone better. He was sure the curvaceous beauty had a lot going for her, but the only thing he remembered being on display were her voluptuous boobs. He'd grown enough in his years since grad school to desire more than just a set of impressive curves. The old Chris would have continued dating her, but recently he found himself wanting something different.

Chris placed the mail back on the desk, when their restaurant manager knocked on the door. Sitting down, he called for her to come in.

"Hey, babycakes." Trina was also the establishment's equal-opportunity flirt. Her tall, shapely frame made it easy for men to receive her harmless advances. She always had an ego-enhancing compliment handy. "How's it going?" Trina sat on the edge of his desk.

"Pretty good. What about you?"

"Just marvelous. I'd be even better had my date ended well last night."

"You too? That seems to be going around."

Trina rolled her eyes. "It's getting harder to find good ones these days. I'm glad Ray found someone that he seems to adore. You and Kent are the last two great catches standing. Too bad I don't date my bosses." Her snicker made Chris laugh. "Anyway, I didn't come to complain about my dating misadventures. A gentleman stopped by to ask about playing a live set. He's a violinist."

Chris narrowed his eyes.

"I know. I told him that we focus on jazz, but then he whipped out his instrument…" Trina paused and let the innuendo hang in the air. She smirked, obviously amused with herself, and then continued. "His violin, that is," she said, winking. "He proceeded to play the most beautiful rendition of the latest release of that hot new R&B artist, Champagne. I had him leave his contact information and then looked him up online." Trina handed Chris the musician's card. "He's a-*mazing*!" Her eyes rolled back, emphasizing her appreciation for the man's work. "He's pretty popular for his creative renditions of songs, from pop to jazz to classical. I'd love to have him come in and give us a preview, but I wanted to run it by you guys first."

Nodding his head, Chris turned the card between his fingers. "Thanks. Set it up. How's everything else?"

"Outstanding! Also, I received another call from that magazine editor. She's scheduling interviews and photo shoots with the honorees and wanted to get the three of you on her calendar."

"Really!" Chris's brows lifted, and a smile swept across his face. "Check with Kent and Ray, and let's settle on a date soon."

"Cool. You deserve the recognition. You three are doing a great job at making The Reserve a hot spot. It happened so fast."

"Thanks, Trina!" He grinned with a modest amount of pride.

Tilting her head, Trina gave Chris a delightful smile. "Seriously. I'm very proud of you guys." She patted his hand. "And I'm happy to be a part of the team."

"You *are* part of this. Thanks for all you do."

"You're welcome, babycakes. See you at the staff meeting. This girl has some real work to do. I can't just stand around being pretty." She blew a kiss as she left the office.

Things were going well for Chris—the family business, their foundation and this fairly new venture with his longtime friends. Every area of his life seemed to be thriving with a flowing momentum. Dating was the only aspect that was still uncertain. Recently he hadn't met women he was interested in seeing beyond the first few dates. His access to beautiful ladies was still plentiful, but lately most seemed interested in his pedigree. He was over women who wanted him to be attached to the Chandler legacy. Something was changing, and Chris wasn't sure if it was the women or him.

Ray entered their office with the force of a hurricane. "What's up?" His energy charged the room.

"You're here early," Kent kidded, walking in behind him.

"It's three o'clock." Ray's brows furrowed.

"Yeah. On time is early for you!" Chris jumped in on the joke, sharing a laugh with Kent.

"Ha!" Ray clapped his hands. "Let's get this party started." He removed his suit jacket, tossed it on the back of his chair and sat down with his feet up on the desk.

Kent plopped in his chair and swiveled to face Ray. "You seem happy. What's good?"

"Everything!"

Chris laughed, shaking his head. "How's Brynn?"

Ray's smile nearly split his face at the mention of his girlfriend's name. "Brynn's good. I just left her."

"I still can't believe you two met online. I've always been skeptical of that." Chris shrugged, reaching for a notepad.

"Me too, man," Kent agreed.

"I was too, until I found Brynn. I can't believe our paths never crossed before—especially after discovering that we knew so many of the same people. I keep telling you guys to give this online thing a try."

"Maybe I should!" Chris said jokingly. "Do you think it would stop my mother from trying to hook me up with her friends' daughters?"

"Dates chosen by mothers never work out well." Kent chuckled.

"Try it. What can it hurt?" Ray asked.

"It's just not for me." Chris sucked air through his teeth.

"Sounds to me like regular dating isn't working out so well either."

"Very funny, Ray!"

"He's got a point, Chris. We're the ones who are still single."

"By choice," Chris said pointedly, with a lifted index finger.

"Exactly! That's because you've already dated most of the women you know, player!" Kent howled. "Save some for the rest of us, man."

Laughing, Kent offered Ray a high five.

"I can't help it if I'm in demand." Chris gave his collar a smug tug.

Kent and Ray looked at each other and burst into laughter once again. Chris couldn't help but join them. The irony was evident. As eligible a bachelor as he was, his options were narrowing.

"You may have a point, Ray. Maybe it's time for Chris and me to look outside our usual circles. This can be a way to meet new women. It's not as creepy as it used to be. Some pretty decent relationships started online—like yours."

"See? It's not so bad, Chris. Brynn isn't crazy at all." Ray's comment generated another round of laughs.

"Trina said *Eclipse* magazine called. The editor wants to set up an interview." Chris was happy to change the subject. He had too many reservations about this online thing, and he also had a reputation—no, a legacy—to protect.

What would a Chandler look like, searching for a mate online? He didn't express his thoughts aloud in order not to offend Ray. Chris, Ray and Kent had been close friends since high school. Finding beautiful women to date had never been an issue for any of them, so when Ray said that he was trying the online thing, Chris and Kent were shocked. They teased Ray through the entire process but shut their mouths when he introduced them to Brynn. Not only was she beautiful but also grounded, intelligent and apparently completely sane. Kent asked if she had a sister, cousin or mother that he could date. After that, Kent was open to online dating, but Chris still had his reservations.

Chris joined the others in swiping through the calendars on their phones.

"I can do next Wednesday." Kent spoke first. "What time do they want to interview us?"

"Do they want us to come to their offices in the city, or will they come here? That will help me figure out what's best. My calendar is looking a little crazy right now." Ray shook his head. "But I'll be in the city already on Wednesday so, if they want us to meet there, that might work."

"I'll have Trina call and ask. Should we leave Wednesday open either way? Does that work for you?" Chris directed his question toward Ray. His phone was cupped in his hand with his thumb hovering over the screen. Ray nodded. "Cool," Chris continued. "We can let Trina know at the meeting."

"So, fellas. We have a big night coming up tonight, huh?" Ray clapped his hands and rubbed them back and forth.

"Yes, we do!" Chris agreed. "This place is going to be packed. Alfonzo Blackwell is a huge draw."

"How'd you get him again, Chris?" Kent asked.

"He's an old friend of Jewel's. She called in a favor." Chris turned to Ray. "Brynn joining us tonight?"

"For sure! She wouldn't miss a chance to see Blackwell play."

There was that gleam again. Whenever Brynn's name flitted into the atmosphere, Ray appeared lighter—his smile instinctual as if it generated from somewhere well beyond his lips. Chris wondered what that felt like. He thought he had come close in grad school. He figured he had loved Danielle but couldn't recall feeling what Ray seemed to feel, which appeared to transcend emotions and come alive in their very presence.

"You really like this girl." With his head tilted, Chris said those words as if the weight of them had just landed on him. His friend was in love.

Ray sat back in his chair, smiled and exhaled as if the air he released carried away every problem. "I think she's the one."

Chris's and Kent's mouths fell open. They looked at one another and then at Ray.

"Whoa!" Kent held his hands up. "You think so, man?"

An assured nod.

With hands in the air, Chris made a few attempts to speak, closed his mouth and shrugged. His hands fell to his side with a slap. "What can I say? I'm happy for you, man. I have to admit, happiness looks good on you."

"Thanks! One down and two to go." Ray raised his brow.

Kent held up a palm. "Hey! Don't speak so fast. I'm still having fun."

Chris laughed with them but stayed mute. He liked what he saw in Ray, and a part of him wanted to know what that felt like. He just wasn't sure if he'd find it online.

# Chapter 3

Serenity took the dress the attendant handed to her and looked it over. She'd lost the weight but wondered how the dress would actually fit. Peeking at the size, she heard the woman say, "Don't be concerned about that. European sizing is quite different."

That gave her small comfort. The number on the tag was what she wore after losing her first twenty pounds.

"Try it on. I can't wait to see it on you!" Rayne nudged Serenity toward the fitting room. "And you try on this one, Elisa." Their friend took the second dress and nodded her approval. "We'll see which one looks best, and the two of you can choose."

"Let's do this!" Elisa lifted her eyebrows at Serenity.

"Let's do it!"

Serenity stepped into the narrow box of a room and closed the door. Leaning against the wall, she took a deep breath. She'd lost a total of forty pounds so far, and trying on clothes was still a chore because of her curves. People told her all the time how amazing she looked. She received their compliments graciously, but their enthusiasm made her wonder what they were really saying about how she looked before. Her confidence had never been tied to her dress size. But now people treated her differently, especially men, and she wasn't sure she liked that. Inside she was exactly the same person.

Slipping into the dress, Serenity appreciated how the inside layer, with its comfortable elasticity, glided over her curves, yet also fit her waist. The top layer was the same champagne hue but made of lace. The dress settled just off her shoulders, and at the bottom a slight train caressed the floor behind her as she moved. Twisting side to side in the mirror, Serenity smiled, taking a calm breath. It was a good fit. Maybe she didn't need to lose those last ten pounds. Her and her mother's new lifestyle had already proven beneficial to their health and their shapes.

Stepping out of the fitting room, Serenity was met with gasps from her friends and strangers.

"Oh my goodness!" Both of Rayne's hands covered her mouth. "You look absolutely gorgeous."

Elisa stepped out of her fitting room with the champagne halter dress that Rayne had handed to her. "We're wearing that dress." She pointed to Serenity. "Turn around, girl." She took Serenity by the hand, and led her in a ballerina twirl. "This is it, Rayne. What do you think?"

"Stunning! But it's up to you, ladies. Your dress is pretty too, Elisa."

"Uh-huh? Do you see how you said that? I think I prefer *stunning* over *pretty*!" Elisa called to their attendant. "Can you please bring that dress in my size? Thank you so much."

The girls laughed excitedly as the attendant quickly obliged. Elisa disappeared into the fitting room and emerged moments later, looking just as stunning as Serenity.

"We've got our dresses!" Serenity squealed, slapping Elisa high five.

"And I know just where to find the perfect shoes. Now let's go eat. Ha!" Elisa dashed back to her room.

Serenity took one last look at herself from varied angles offered by the multitude of mirrors and headed back to her fitting room, carrying a healthy dose of pride. When the doctor had warned her mother of possible impending diabetes, it had scared both of them. Serenity had supported her mom by changing her eating habits too. They had started out taking walks in the evening and eventually began jogging. Each month they tried something new, so they wouldn't get bored with working out. Now they could both credit yoga, Pilates, kickboxing, boot camp and Pure Barre classes for better health and fit bodies.

An hour later, the girls were chatting over drinks in one of their favorite Thai restaurants.

"That was fun! At least there were no tears this time." Elisa laughed. "We were such a mess when you found your dress, Rayne."

"She looked so beautiful!" Serenity said, with a reminiscent tilt and shake of her head.

"She absolutely *glowed*. I could have sworn I heard harps playing in that bridal shop when she walked out of that dressing room. Ethan is going lose his mind when he sees you on your wedding day."

"Thank you. The moment I stepped into that dress, I knew it was the one." Rayne paused and sipped her ginger martini. "Girls!" Elisa and Serenity looked up. "I'm getting married!" she sang. Rayne closed her eyes and squealed, flapping her hands in the air. Elisa and Serenity squealed along with her. "I can't believe it!"

The shrieks snagged the attention of the few patrons

in the restaurant. Most smiled, signing off on their happy display.

Laughing, Rayne shrunk into her shoulders. "Sorry," she said to her collective audience.

"I love Ethan. From the moment I met him, he became the big brother I never had." Serenity leaned left to allow the waiter to place her sushi on the table.

"I know. You did good, girl." Elisa winked.

"Speaking of Ethan, he asked about your date the other night. He laughed when I told him how horrific you said it was." Rayne hid her smile behind the martini glass, sipped and stretched her eyes at Serenity.

"Tell him I said it went like this…" Serenity put one hand over her throat and, with the other, she pretended to stick a finger into her mouth. The spectacle made Elisa cover her mouth to keep the wine she drank from spraying the table. Rayne, with her hand over her heart and her head back, laughed so hard she snorted, which propelled the girls into a frenzy of laughter until tears streaked their faces.

"Oh—" Rayne tried to catch her breath "—I can't believe I just did that!"

Serenity's sides ached. She panted in an attempt to pull herself together. Each time they calmed down, they would start all over again.

"That's why I love hanging with you, ladies," Elisa said. "We can be totally silly. Clint doesn't get it." She referred to her boyfriend. "I told him that his friends didn't know how to really have fun."

"I know. Ethan thinks we're nuts too. And when I get home, I'm going to show him just what Serenity thought about that date." Chuckles spread around the table once again. "Seriously, he actually hoped it would work out."

"I know. Just let him know I'm no longer interested in his matchmaking services."

"If we leave it up to you, your next date is likely to be with a floormate at your nursing home!" Elisa said matter-of-factly, before tossing a spicy tuna roll in her mouth.

Serenity's mouth opened and closed. "What?"

"You always say you don't have time to date."

"She's right." Rayne nodded her head vigorously. "That's why Ethan has been on the case, trying to hook you up with his friends and colleagues."

"I'd make time for the right one." Serenity squared her shoulders.

"When?" Elisa and Rayne said at the same time.

"Whatever!" Serenity waved her hand, dismissing their interrogation. Of course she didn't have an answer. Up until recently, she hardly thought about dating. Work and the organization occupied her time and thoughts. "I just don't have a lot of spare time."

"We always make time for what we want," Rayne challenged.

"Besides, what kid are you giving music lessons to at eight o'clock on a Saturday night?" Elisa said.

Having no viable answer, Serenity playfully rolled her eyes at Elisa. "It's not that I'm not open to dating. It's just…not easy finding a nice guy. The last few that I went out with were complete disasters. Most of them just want to have sex and text. I want long conversations on the phone. I want to learn a few things about a man before I jump into bed with him…like his STD status. Ha!" All three fell out laughing.

"That's funny but so true." Elisa punctuated her statement with a fork in Serenity's direction. "I agree."

"Seriously. It seems like men don't want to take their

time to get to know women these days. I'm kind of an old-fashioned girl. I want to be courted."

"You're right, Serenity. I think that's why I fell for Ethan. He didn't pressure me to sleep with him on the first date like some other guys I dated. We spent time getting to know and really like each other. We're friends."

"That's what I want! Someone willing to be my friend."

"It's so important. I believe that the friendship that Ethan and I have will get us through the rough spots that are sure to come up. Without friendship as a foundation, what can a couple stand on when a little turbulence hits the relationship?"

"Exactly." Serenity sat up straighter. "Think about it. Most friendships outlast relationships. Have you ever wondered why?"

Elisa slowly nodded her head in consideration. "You're right. Some of my friendships, like ours, date back to childhood."

"And before Clint, you didn't have a relationship that lasted more than two years!" Serenity saw the realization dawning in Elisa's eyes. "That's because friendships play by a different set of rules. We accept our friends for who they are, regardless of how great or zany they may be, but we look for people to date who will conform to our expectations of them. It's not fair. If we treated our relationships more like friendships, maybe they would last just as long."

"Whoa! Look at you giving solid relationship advice." Rayne nudged Elisa. "Did you hear that?"

"She's absolutely right." Elisa nodded in agreement.

"The real question is, how do I find a great friend that could become a great boyfriend?"

"You should try one of those online dating sites so you can expand your options," Elisa offered.

Serenity's head reared back. She jerked into a rigid upright position. "Not with all those crazy people! No way! Do you want me to come up missing?"

"Serenity," Rayne almost pleaded, "I know plenty of people who met online and even got married. It's not like it used to be. Everyone does it these days. There's nothing to be afraid of."

Serenity shook her head and wagged her finger. "Those people lie. They'll post a profile picture that looks like Denzel and, when you meet them in person, they look more like the Hunchback of Notre Dame. No. No. No."

"Since you don't get out much, it could be convenient for you. Bypass the profiles of any you don't like. That way you won't have to waste time going out on bad dates. If you find someone, we won't let you go on the date alone. Rayne and I will be there, lurking...watching." Elisa shaded her eyes with her hand and bent forward, pretending to spy. "We'll make sure he's not Quasimodo in disguise."

"I don't know about this." Serenity pressed her lips together and took a deep breath.

"I've done it," Rayne admitted, waving off Serenity's objection as if it were no big deal.

"Me too." Elisa shrugged. "Met a few cuties too. Nothing panned out, but it wasn't because they looked like Quasimodo and shouted *'Sanctuary!'* when we went out."

Serenity's laugh caught her off guard. She sipped water to push down a piece of rice that had caught in her throat.

"I didn't know you had both dated people you met online."

"Remember Don? The guy I dated before Ethan?"

"Oh, yes! You *did* meet him online. I totally forgot about that. Remember how nervous I was when you went on your first date with him? I tried to talk you out of going."

"Yes, you made me give you my log-in information so you could track my phone."

"No!" Elisa said in disbelief. "Serenity, you really did that?"

"Sure did!"

Elisa reached across the table. "Give me your phone. We can download an app and sign you up to one of the sites right now."

"Yes!" Rayne cheered.

"No!"

"Try it out for a few days. Check out the guys and, if you still don't feel comfortable, just delete your profile and account. I think if you see what it's really like, you might be a little more comfortable with it. Right, Rayne?"

"Just give it a try, Serenity."

After a long pause, Serenity slid her phone over to Elisa with a grunt.

"Okay. Let me show you how to do it." Elisa scooted closer to Serenity.

The three peered at the phone together as Elisa explained the differences between the various sites. Serenity picked one, and watched as Elisa downloaded the app. Elisa typed the answers to the questions on the site as Serenity provided the responses. She then instructed Serenity to pick a selfie that she really liked for her profile picture. It wasn't long before the profile was complete.

"All done." Elisa presented Serenity's phone to her.

She took back her phone as if it were an unfamiliar object. "I can't believe I let you talk me into this." What had she just agreed to?

# Chapter 4

Chris dragged himself into his luxury condominium. One of the few high-rise structures of its kind on Long Island. He loved the charged atmosphere of the city but didn't want to deal with its noisy, restless backdrop the entire night. His condo offered the best of both worlds, with modern city-like living in a serene, suburban setting, but without the steady buzz of people and honking of car horns. He'd kept his place in Manhattan to hang out there when he had to handle business or had grown too tired to make it back home.

Tossing his keys onto the antique side table by the door, Chris trudged into his sleek kitchen to grab a bottle of water. Moonlight filtered through the glass walls in the living room, casting an amber glow throughout the spacious apartment. Propped against the white marble countertop, he nearly drained the water in one long gulp. He set the almost-empty bottle down, closed his eyes and took a deep breath.

Moments from the evening flashed in his mind's eye and a smile eased across his lips. The Reserve had been packed to the gills. He perfectly recalled the pop of corks,

the hum of voices and rumble of laughter that had filled
the space. Blackwell's performance had been stellar. He
had breathed life into his sax, capturing the audience
in a melodic trance. Collectively, fingers tapped, heads
bobbed and the small area where Trina suggested they
keep clear of tables and chairs was filled with dancing
couples. At one point, the audience urged Chris's eldest
sister, Chloe, to join Alfonzo onstage for a duet—her
voice and his sax had joined and floated soulfully through
the air, lifting everyone with them. By the time they were
done, Chris felt like the floor was miles below his feet.
The staff hadn't had a free moment all night, but by the
time they had left, they were all happily exhausted.

Chris sniffed a chuckle, remembering the gorgeous
blonde who had kept flirting with him. Her green eyes
sparkled and her voice dipped an octave, emerging sexy
and seductive through honey-colored lips that were made
perfectly plump by injections. She had zeroed in on him
and he had enjoyed every ounce of the sweet attention
she poured over him like molasses. He'd fought the urge
to lick his lips when she smiled. He'd begun to wonder
what their first date would be like, until she shared that
she had just had to meet him when she'd found out he was
one of the owners. His excitement shut off like a light.
He wondered if she would have given him the same attention if he'd just been a patron. These small indications
of superficiality were fast becoming turnoffs.

In his distinctly charming manner, Chris had eased
out of her magnetic hold without chipping at her dignity.
He had told her how beautiful she was, which wasn't a
lie. With a soft touch slightly above her lower back, he
had leaned close to her ear and expressed how he had
enjoyed talking to her but unfortunately needed to get
back to work. He had thanked her sincerely for patron-

izing The Reserve and had mentioned that he hoped she and her friends would come again. With a kiss to the back of her hand, he had bid her a wonderful evening and departed, backing away slowly, smiling, without false promises. She had got the message and pouted, seeming a little disappointed, but smiled seductively, still with an arch in her long neck and a bare shoulder pushed forward. She had winked, slid a finger across her lips and said good-night before sauntering away and joining her friends at their table. As he moved around throughout the night, he had caught her staring several times. She'd pout, smile and allow her lustful gaze to linger for seconds before turning away.

Chris finished off the water and tossed the bottle into the recycling bin. Despite being tired, he was still too wound up to sleep and figured a long, hot shower would help him relax. Picking up the remote, he turned off the lights in the kitchen and living room and headed toward his bedroom. Walking through the closet, he pulled boxers from a drawer and continued to the bathroom for the shower. Emerging clean and smelling like mint, he slipped into his underwear and flopped onto the bed, ready for a comforting night of sleep.

A half hour later, the anticipated slumber still hadn't come. Chris picked up his phone and started scrolling through pictures on The Reserve's Facebook page. So many people had posted about the night's performance. Others posted everything from pictures of their food to wine choices to selfies outside with the name on the awning in the background. The blonde had even added a comment to a posted picture about how much she had enjoyed herself and had to come back soon.

Seeing the woman's picture made him think about the theme common to the women he'd been meeting lately.

Chris hesitated a moment, letting his finger hover over the screen of his phone. After a moment he touched the icon that brought up a search engine. He laughed at himself. Was he really considering this? He entered *dating sites* into the search bar. Several of them came up, as well as options for apps that he could download on his phone. After perusing the list for about ten minutes, he settled on one of the apps that, based on its description, didn't seem so intrusive. It offered local prospects, which seemed reasonable. He never thought he'd do well in long-distance relationships.

Chris downloaded the app and started putting together a profile using the name Chris Mullins. He completed every swipe, upload, and tap of a letter with trepidation. He selected a full-body picture so that his facial features wouldn't be as prominent. His thumb hovered over the image. Once that finger connected with the screen, his profile would become visible to a vast pool of companion seekers. He hated to think that this would make him seem desperate. He tried to bear in mind the reassurance of his friends.

Chris had never been the kind to follow the herd, but this time, knowing that many others had searched for mates online seemed comforting. He wasn't alone in this. He wasn't the first. This would expand his options. He personally knew someone who had succeeded in finding a great woman online. Convincing himself worked. He touched the screen, making his profile public. It was official.

He sat up in bed and, resting against the headboard, closed his eyes. Letting out a deep sigh and then a grunt, he blew out his concerns. This couldn't hurt him. In fact, it could prove to be interesting—fun, even. He didn't have to commit to anything or anyone. He considered it a new method of blind dating, with the benefit of seeing what your date looked like before you actually met. Curiosity captured his focus as he thought about the possibilities.

He swiped through a few profile pictures, surprised at how many attractive women he found there, but wondered if the images they posted were depictions of what they really looked like.

"Ha!" Chris released a hearty laugh into the silence that enveloped his room. What if he got catfished? That would certainly make for a good story with the guys.

Reading through profiles, he formed a few opinions. There were several options for filtering his search, such as location, interests and ethnicity. The site offered a smorgasbord of women, featuring every type of personality. This he determined much from the pictures alone, which showed women in everything from business suits to minuscule bikinis that advertised all their major "assets." He did come across one or two that he was tempted to send private messages to but seemed to be at a loss for what to say. That never happened when he was in front of a woman in real life.

Chris laughed at himself again. He still wasn't one hundred percent sure about this, but he was now official. He was in the game despite his reservations. Connecting his phone to the charger, he lay back down on the bed and pulled the covers up to his neck. Nestling into his memory-foam mattress, he thought about the possibilities until his lids grew heavy enough to shut out all thoughts.

# Chapter 5

Serenity's phone buzzed. She snatched it off the desk with one ferocious motion. Holding the phone against her chest, she felt it vibrate slightly at the same rapid pace of her heart. She didn't know how much longer she'd keep that app on her phone. The constant notifications ran her battery down, but curiosity wouldn't allow her to mute the alerts. With each buzz, a burst of air radiated in her stomach, sending nervous tremors through her core. Closing her eyes, she took a deep breath and exhaled. She looked up at the clock. She had three minutes before the third-period bell rang and a herd of seventh graders would come charging into the music room.

Entering the passcode on her screen, she opened the dating app. She had more private messages, one from a gentleman who looked like her favorite uncle. She scrunched her nose and deleted his message without reading it. She hadn't actually read any of the messages fully. She only saw part of the first line, which was previewed under the subject line. She didn't know if the sender could tell if she had opened the messages or not. Instead she let them pile up, reducing the likelihood of responding. She clicked on a few more profiles.

Despite her reservations, she was entertained by what people wrote in their profiles. Some kept their introductory lines simple, describing their interests and professions. Others got creative. She stopped short at the profile of a good-looking caramel-colored man with a smooth black goatee, assuming she'd be intrigued by his summary. Instead, what she found caused abrupt laughter to erupt from her mouth.

"You've got to be kidding!"

She read the words under his picture again.

*Roses are red, violets are tan,*
*You finally found your perfect man.*

Giggling, she took a screenshot of his profile with the cheesy poem and tapped a quick text to her girlfriends on their group chat and uploaded the image.

This is why online dating is a bad idea! LOL!

That text would serve as a source of amusement for the rest of their day. Returning to the dating app and shaking her head, she closed the window of his profile. The next one featured a full-body picture of what looked like a rather handsome man. Serenity zoomed in to see his face better. His summary said he loved music, travel and great wines. The information he provided was minimal, and for some reason that intrigued her. She looked at his zip code and realized that he was also from Nassau County.

The school bell rang long and piercingly. She flinched, launching from her seat. One hand flew to her chest, while the other tightened the grip on her cell phone to keep it from flying out of her hand. In that short amount of time, she'd forgotten where she was.

"Goodness!" She recovered her breath, sighed and opened the music-room door. The second bell rang, and students poured from classrooms, filling the halls with a high volume of chatter.

"Hey, Ms. Williams."

"Hey, Melanie."

Serenity held her hand up for Melanie and her other students to slap her high five. Some of the crowd carried their loud chatter from the hallway into her classroom. Girls snickered, boys laughed, friends promised to meet after class.

The next forty-three minutes would take her mind off the dating site. Serenity was thankful for the reprieve. She was curious about the man named Chris Mullins. She pushed him to the back of her mind and closed the door.

"Okay, everyone. Settle down, take your seats and take out your music books. We're going to start by reading notes. We're learning a new song today. Turn to page two-fourteen."

"Sing for us, Ms. Williams," one of her students called out.

"Open your books, guys." Serenity smiled and shook her head. She loved everything about music, and she would sing or play one of several instruments for her class when they behaved well.

*"Please?"* students chorused.

"Yes, Ms. Williams. *Please?*"

"You promised!"

"I did?" She scanned the room with a skeptical gaze.

"Yes. You said if all of us handed in our papers on time that you'd sing for us next class."

"Okay, okay."

Serenity walked over to the piano, sat down, opened one of the music books and flipped through the pages.

They loved when she taught them how to play popular music—especially songs from their favorite artists. "Turn to page ninety-six in your music books. I'll start singing and, those who know how to play the song, join me on the chorus."

Their response was collective. One student pumped his trumpet in the air.

Serenity cleared her throat, and the room fell into absolute silence. Delicately she fingered the intro on the piano keys and began singing the first verse to one of the most popular songs on the radio.

"Yeah, Ms. W!"

Serenity laughed but didn't break her flow. She was a good singer but a better musician. Some students snapped their fingers. Others waved. One stood and pretended to dance with an imaginary partner. Serenity chuckled at his dramatic display but relished the fact that her students appreciated her talent and loved music as much as she did.

She held one hand high, lifting a finger, signaling her students of the upcoming chorus. Without missing a beat, she raised her eyebrows. The students took that as their cue and lifted their instruments in preparation. After four head nods from her, they joined in, undergirding her voice with their harmonies. Once the class picked up the rhythm, Serenity stood, still singing, pushing deeper into the song, now feeling it on the inside.

Walking the tempo, she made her way around the room, careful to acknowledge each student with a smile or wink. She made her way back to the front by the time she released the last note into the air, holding it long enough for her students to stop playing, stand and begin cheering.

"Oh my gosh, Ms. Williams! That was amazing."

"So dope," one young man said.

Her smile radiated from her core. She curtsied, taking in her adoring students' applause.

"Okay, now. Let's get to work."

"Okay," someone whined.

Serenity guided them through their lesson. As usual the class came to a rapid end—the bell ringing while they were still playing.

"Okay—" Serenity clapped and shouted over the varying sounds of the instruments "—we're done. Don't forget to pick up a permission slip on my desk for the show. Make sure a parent signs them. Remember, your artist profiles are due next time."

Quickly, the students replaced their instruments in their cases and stacked them in closets. The class was completely cleared seconds after the second bell.

Serenity plopped into her chair feeling both exhilarated and winded. Teaching took so much energy but gave her so much joy. She had a free period, which she planned to spend preparing for her next group. Wheeling her chair snugly into the opening of her desk, she tapped the space bar on the computer, bringing the screen to life. Her phone buzzed. She'd temporarily forgotten about the dating app, but now it would dominate her focus again.

Just as she picked up the phone, Rayne rapped on the door two quick times before stepping in.

"How's it going?"

"Great! They made me sing again."

"That's because they love you."

"I guess so."

"Give any more thought to the dating app?" Rayne sat on the corner of the desk and plucked a mini candy bar from the dish Serenity kept there.

Serenity shrunk into her shoulders. "Yeah."

"You did?" Rayne's eyes opened as wide as her gaping mouth. "Cool!"

Serenity rolled her eyes. "Don't make such a big deal about it. I just perused some of the profiles."

"Oh! See anything you like?" Rayne lifted a brow and popped the unwrapped candy in her mouth. Balling up the shiny cover, she shot it toward the wastepaper basket as if she were going for a layup.

"Nice shot."

"*So.* Any prospects?"

"Not quite yet. I did see a few cute guys though. Some are nuts, just like I anticipated."

"Oh my goodness! I laughed so hard at that horrible poem you sent. Did that guy message you?"

"He and a bunch of others, but I haven't responded to anyone yet."

"Why not?"

Serenity shrugged and sat back in her chair. "I need to get more comfortable with this first." Her mind shifted to the image of Chris Mullins again. She wondered what else was in his profile, but the old-fashioned girl in her refused to let her believe that pursuing him was a good idea. She wasn't sure how to apply the dating rules to all this online stuff, nor did she know if she was willing to make the first move.

"All right. Keep me posted. I need to go grade some essays." Rayne slid off the desk. "I'll see you later, right?"

"Of course. Would I miss Elisa's birthday dinner? Actually, the real question is, would I miss the duck confit appetizer at Gem?"

"Or that beautiful black rice. Yum!"

"Ha! You're making my mouth water." Serenity looked at her watch. "I haven't even had lunch yet."

"Remember to keep it light."

"I will, so I can have room for all that deliciousness later tonight." Serenity rubbed her belly. "I think it was a good idea for Clint to surprise her with a dinner today instead of on the weekend. I'm sure Elisa isn't expecting us to be there."

"I know. She thinks we're going out Friday instead. I can't wait to see her face." Rayne started for the door. "Later, lady." She tossed a wave over her shoulder as she exited.

"Later."

Serenity gathered the remaining permission slips on her desk, neatened them and tapped the bottom of the pile against the desktop to line them up. She placed them in a manila folder and set it in a tray. Her phone buzzed. She looked at it, paused and returned to what she was doing. She picked up the pile of homework her students had handed in and began reading the summaries on the history of jazz. She glanced at the phone once more. This time, it didn't buzz.

The first few lines of the first summary she had started hadn't made sense, so she read it over again. The work wasn't poorly written. She just couldn't concentrate on her students' papers because her mind was on the messages in the app.

"That's it!" she declared. "This app is making me crazy." What was the use if she didn't plan on checking any of the messages anyway?

Serenity snatched the phone, tapped in her passcode, then held the app down so she could open and then delete it. Pausing again, she was compelled to review the profiles one last time. After that, she'd be done with it. Just then a new message arrived in her inbox. It was from Chris Mullins. The subject simply said Hello. It was the first line that caught her attention, so she clicked on it to bring up the full message. This Chris didn't call her baby, write a bad poem or offer up a lame pick-up line. His message was simple.

Hi. It seems that you really like music. Do you play any instruments? I play the sax.

Serenity's thumb hovered over the reply icon for several moments. The debate in her mind was whether or not she should respond, or back out and hit Delete. The pressure was palpable. Why was she making this a big deal? Her reservations mounted. What if he was a stalker? He could be misrepresenting himself. Maybe he was crazy. Why was she even using online dating?

This guy looked decent enough. He was pretty handsome in the one and only picture he posted—and he was fully clothed. There were no pecs, six-packs or weird, phony-looking model poses. His profile was new, like hers—simple.

"I can't," Serenity said to herself, sighing, and dropped her hands.

She opened the bottom desk drawer, unzipped her purse and tossed the phone in. It would stay there for the remainder of her workday.

# Chapter 6

Chris, Ray and Kent navigated the congested streets of New York's busy Times Square area with confidence in their stride. Tourists strolled aimlessly with their eyes toward the sky, while agitated natives wound through the maze of people speaking a tapestry of dialects. Chris caught snatches of the few languages he understood and wondered about the ones he couldn't detect.

Broadway—the street—was a show unto itself. Entrance into the theaters wasn't necessary for theatrics. There was enough of that with the costumed characters walking around and encouraging people to take pictures with them, then wanting money. The area was littered with painted naked women, superheroes, Statues of Liberty on stilts and metallic-toned cowboys who held their breath for dollars.

"Here we are." Kent stopped walking, looked up at the large silver numbers on the building and shielded his eyes from the glaring sun.

The three headed through stately glass doors into a well-lit lobby of slate-colored granite, with a long security desk featuring a chrome logo of the media conglomerate's name. A woman sat at the desk, her lips easing into a delightful grin when they approached. Eager to assist, she caught their attention before her coworker could turn around.

Chris stepped up first, gave his name and then the name of the person they were scheduled to meet. The woman asked for their identification and directed them to the elevator that would take them to where they needed to go. Inside the office, a petite young woman greeted them, leading them down a hall lined with large mounted posters of magazine covers. She guided them into a cozy room with soothing sage walls, gray couches and shabby-chic decor. Her gaze lingered on Chris as he moved through the door. After inviting them to get comfortable, she left.

"This is going to be great for business," Ray mentioned, taking in the view overlooking Times Square from several stories up.

"For sure!" Kent agreed. "When will this issue come out, again?"

"May, around the same time as the gala." Chris sat and brushed imaginary lint off his pant leg.

Had he been completely honest with his buddies, Chris would have told them how nervous he was. He was no stranger to attention, nor had he ever required it, but this entire experience humbled him tremendously, setting his ego into remission. It felt great to be recognized for work that he loved. He was still processing the fact that the three of them were about to be interviewed for a cover story of one of the country's largest lifestyle magazines. Their feature story would tell the world about their business venture and their quick rise to popularity, giving them exponential exposure. Chris would also be featured in a separate article as one of New York's most eligible bachelors, which would also tell of him being honored for his contribution and service as the cochair of the board for the Chandler Foundation alongside his mother. Each of his siblings took turns serving with Elle except Jade, his younger sister, who currently served as the foundation's executive director.

Ray and Chris sat while Kent paced the small tranquil space. The nervous energy he exuded contrasted with the serenity the room offered. Chris laughed, realizing Kent shared the same mental space.

"You're not nervous?" Chris directed his question to Ray.

Ray rubbed his palms against his legs. "Yeah, man. This is some major exposure. Brynn came by this morning before work. She kept fussing over what outfit she wanted me to wear. I told her the magazine was supplying our clothes for the shoot anyway. She still insisted that I show up looking as dapper as usual. Heh!" Ray confidently popped his collar. "I'll try not to make you two look bad."

"Ha!" Their combined laughter filled the small space.

Moments later, the editor entered the room. With hair the color of fire, her kinks evenly extended about six inches from her head. Smooth, almond-colored skin looked like butter. Her big smile was inviting.

"Good morning, gentlemen. I'm Chandra, business editor. Welcome to *Eclipse* magazine. It's such a pleasure to finally meet you in person." She firmly shook hands with each.

"A pleasure to meet you." Ray nodded.

"Thank you for this opportunity." Kent smiled. "Whoa!" he teased regarding her firm handshake. "You've got some arm there."

"I think it's safe to say the pleasure is ours." Chris

cupped Chandra's soft hand between his. "And yes, thanks so much for this opportunity."

Chandra's neck shifted like a lever as she swallowed. She cleared her throat and smiled. Her smile held a hint of seduction and turned inviting. Chris could tell she thought he was flirting, but he wasn't.

"You're quite charming, Mr. Chandler." Chandra's head tilted slightly.

"Thank you." Aware of his effect, he patted the back of her hand and let it go.

Chandra cleared her throat once again and tugged her knee-length dress down. "Our team is preparing for your shoot. We'll get started in a moment. In the meantime, please let me know if you need anything. We have refreshments for you and a wonderful lunch coming later."

"Now you're talking." Kent rubbed his hands together.

Chandra laughed, then stole a glance at Chris before promising to send in her assistant with a few bottles of water as she left.

"Seems like she's sweet on you, Chris." Ray chuckled and looked to Kent to cosign.

"Yeah, I'd say so. Maybe you won't need that dating site after all."

"Right! Very funny!" Chris dismissed Kent's comment with a wave.

He hadn't thought about his profile on the dating site since he asked that woman about her musical interests. Suddenly he was curious to see if she had responded but didn't want to check it in front of his buddies. They were sure to joke about it.

Out of all the women whose profiles he had perused, there was something honest about the one belonging to the woman who spoke about having a passion for teaching music. The fact that he was attracted to her authenticity was ironic, since his profile consisted of a few lies—well, the last name and city he had listed were lies. But he did play the sax and trumpet, and he was an entrepreneur. He just hadn't mentioned the businesses he owned or anything about his family's legacy.

The assistant returned, snapping Chris out of his daze. They were ready to get them set up for their photo shoot. After that, he'd check to see if she'd responded to his message. Chris was surprised at his own desire to see if she had.

## Chapter 7

Serenity hit her doorstep with the weight of her entire day pulling her down. She'd listened to more than one hundred students play instruments with varying levels of skill. Some instruments shrieked and shrilled, forcing one of her eyes to close while the other widened from the harsh sounds. With an endearing smile, she had encouraged them to continue and told them how much they were improving. Most of the musicians in her upper grades played beautifully due to several years of practice.

After school, she had headed over to the community center to rehearse with the kids from her organization, Heartstrings. She founded the nonprofit with Rayne to help less-fortunate kids learn to play instruments while developing an appreciation for music and the arts. They managed to acquire donations for instruments and materials. Sometimes they were lucky enough to get visits from prominent musicians who liked what they were doing and wanted to show support.

They had a few months to prepare for their year-end concert. Serenity's heart swelled as she listened to them play on this particular evening. They were especially good, proving that they practiced between sessions. She'd taught them about the ten-thousand-hour rule as a way to develop mastery and expertise. A few of her kids took that very seriously and began practicing diligently, charting the amount of time they spent playing their instruments.

Serenity stepped into her kitchen and flicked the lights on, disturbing the darkness there. She was still smiling as she transitioned her thoughts from her kids to what she wanted to eat for dinner. Opening the refrigerator, she stood scanning each shelf carefully. Finally, she pulled out feta cheese, romaine lettuce, tomatoes and a few other veggies to make her own version of a Greek salad. She washed the produce and left it in a strainer to dry while she showered and slipped into comfy lounge pants, fluffy socks and a T-shirt.

She made her salad, poured a cup of juice and folded herself in her favorite wing chair next to her bed. She loved that chair, which she'd inherited after her grandmother's passing. If she sat still enough, she swore she could feel the warmth that had often radiated from her grandmother.

On a table adjacent to the chair, Serenity tapped a button on a small flat remote, turning on the Bluetooth, and used her phone to select a playlist that released the soothing melodies of instrumentals throughout the cozy space. With the remote, she also turned on the TV, muting the volume, filling the atmosphere with the energy of movement and lights, almost making it seem as if she weren't home alone. That was how she liked it.

Moments later, her phone buzzed, silencing her music for a moment. Serenity picked up the phone and saw that she'd received another alert from the dating app. Once again, her thumb hovered over the app icon, contemplating its deletion. She hesitated long enough for her curiosity to get the upper hand. Thumbing through, she looked over the messages. The one from Chris Mullins stood out. He'd mentioned music.

Serenity opened the message and paused. She dropped her hands into her lap and sighed. Responding to this message would officially put her in the online dating game. *What if he was crazy?* She'd already gone over that in her mind multiple times. She decided to go ahead and answer. Adrenaline rushed to her fingers. They trembled slightly as she positioned her thumbs over the phone's keyboard. Suddenly, she couldn't formulate a sensible reply in her head. How could she be so nervous and this guy wasn't even around? He was simply a figment of a person, on the other side of a digital wall. What could she lose? What could she *win*?

Her fingers moved over the phone like rapid fire, preventing her from thinking too much or talking herself out of answering him back. She wasn't sure of what she'd written until she read it over.

I love music and play several instruments—piano, violin, clarinet and sax also. You seem to be a music lover too.

By the time Serenity wrote, edited, deleted and rewrote that simple message, she found herself breathing hard, as if typing caused her to exert physical energy. She laid the phone on the side table as if it were hot. Then she laughed. She laughed until tears streamed down her face. What was wrong with her? If she acted this way now, how would she act if she actually met this man in person? That would probably never happen, she thought, waving her hand in the air dismissively.

Serenity picked up her bowl and stabbed a hearty fork-

ful of salad. Midway to her mouth, her phone buzzed
again. She paused, steadying the food inches from her
open mouth. Her heart rate quickened. She laid the fork
in the bowl, carefully placed the bowl back on the table
and picked up the phone. As she thought, it was the guy
replying to her.

*That was quick.*

Serenity swiped her way to the message.

Wow! That's cool. How long have you been playing?

That sparked an instant conversation via the in-app
messaging system. Music had always been easy to talk
about. The initial pressure she'd anxiously anticipated had
quickly waned as their conversation continued. Within
the next fifteen minutes, they knew of each other's music-
loving history, favorite musicians and best-rated perfor-
mances. Comfort had sidled its way into their interaction.
The first layer of Serenity's heavily guarded defense system was down. Music was the Trojan horse.

The two exchanged email addresses, taking the conversation offline. Email was as personal as she was willing to get for now. Offering up her cell phone number
wasn't on the table yet. Perhaps that option would come
later, after she'd gotten to know him more—as much as
one could get to know someone via email.

When talk of music was temporarily exhausted, Chris
treaded into a sea of more personal inquiries—but none
too intrusive. He asked about her likes. She told him
about her work teaching music to disadvantaged youth
but carefully withheld the name of her organization and
deliberately failed to mention that she was a founding
partner. He mentioned that he sat on the board of a non-

profit organization that served youth. He too avoided naming his company.

He gives back to his community, Serenity deduced from his board involvement. She figured he was also straddling the line of giving just enough information. Technically they were still strangers, so she was fine with that. The conversation turned to family makeup. Serenity explained that she was an only child, initially raised by a single mother, and that she had always wanted sisters. Chris emailed about his three siblings and large lively family and joked about selling his three sisters to her for a nominal fee.

*Sense of humor—check!* Serenity liked what she seemed to pick up from their exchange. They continued getting to know each other. By the time they ended their email discussion, her curiosity had been thoroughly piqued. He had grown up on the North Shore of Long Island, but she didn't know where he lived now. He had an MBA, managed a hectic schedule like she did and was family-oriented. Both of them enjoyed traveling abroad and had a desire to visit all fifty states. Still, she wanted to know more. But for now, she let him know it had been great "chatting" with him. He promised to reach out again soon.

And he did—the very next night, and then again the night after that.

## Chapter 8

Chris hurried to his car, still dripping with the sweat of his workout. He looked forward to going home, getting on the computer and exchanging emails with Serenity. They had communicated in that fashion every day for the past two weeks. Their conversation always made room for talk about music. He did some research, finding her on social media, and viewed what he could of her profiles without being a connection, friend or follower. He liked what he saw.

Serenity's passion for music and life and her fun-loving nature were the threads woven throughout her online narrative. Chris viewed pictures of her hanging with friends, working with youth and spending time with her mother. One look at the older version of her and he could tell she had inherited her good looks from her mother. Both had beautiful doe eyes that he imagined would compel him to offer her the world with a single bat of her lashes. He learned about her forty-pound weight loss and how it was inspired by her mother's health scare. Before and after pictures chronicling the journey of both women revealed their curvaceous frames prior to dropping the pounds and showed them looking just as gorgeous in new svelte figures after the weight loss.

Chris could already tell that Serenity had a big heart and wondered how she might respond to the fact that he hadn't been completely honest about who he was. Purposely, he never asked to connect with her via social media since he, of course, didn't have any profiles under his partially fictitious name. Chris Mullins was a ghost online. He'd gotten the last name Mullins from his grandparents' hometown in South Carolina. When she had asked him about his online presence, he'd simply said he wasn't a fan of social media and with his busy schedule wasn't sure how he'd find time to engage anyway. Who knew how things would go? Maybe he'd never get the opportunity to even tell her the truth. Yet the more they communicated, the more he wanted to meet her in person. It was quite possible that once they actually spoke or met the intrigue that resulted from only knowing so much about one another would wane. Serenity could be just like the other women he'd been meeting lately. Then he'd be happy that he hadn't got too close. He decided to see how far this could go. He had time before having to worry about his fictitious identity.

The short ride to and from his gym and home seemed even shorter with his mind on Serenity. He made the trip on autopilot, hardly recalling the route he'd taken. Inside, he washed the sweat off his body with a long hot shower, stepped into sweatpants and sat on the bed.

Chris planned to ask for her number. Would her voice sound the way he imagined, based on her pictures? If she were reluctant, he'd move on. Two weeks of email was enough for him.

After settling in, propped against his headboard, Chris turned on his laptop and launched his email.

How was your day?

Chris reached for the remote and brought the television to life while he awaited her response. He had missed the first half of the basketball game. During a commercial, he refreshed his email and saw that she had responded. A smile eased across his lips. She replied with a quick account of how hectic her day had been. The grant application she had to get in before five o'clock, the students she had to settle a conflict with, and the restaurant she and her friend had to check out to see if it was a good choice for their friend's bridal shower.

Chris replied with a few details of his busy day at work and the fact that he was happy that he didn't have to go in to work tonight.

Would it be okay if I called you?

He again wondered what she sounded like. Her reply didn't come instantly like the others. He smiled, imagining her doe eyes looking at his words with trepidation etched in her expression. He'd wait. He got up, headed to the kitchen and popped the top off a bottle of beer. Taking two swigs before leaving the kitchen, he headed back to the bedroom, sat and placed the PC on his lap.

Serenity sent her number. Chris swallowed another swig of beer before reaching for his cell phone. He dialed. She answered on the first ring.

"Hello." Her voice was soft but professional—confident. The sound was pleasing—full and feminine.

"It's nice to hear your voice." He felt himself smile.

"Is it what you thought it would be like?"

"Better."

"Are you flirting with me, Mr. Mullins?"

At first, Chris was thrown. *Mr. Mullins.* He'd never actually been called by his fake name before.

"Maybe. I've wondered what you sounded like. Now that I know, I like what I hear." She was blushing and he could feel it. "Did I make you blush?"

"You know how to put a girl on the spot, don't you?"

"I'm direct."

"I like that."

"Are you flirting with me, Ms. Williams?" Chris teased.

"Maybe."

The two of them laughed. The ice had been broken. They eased into conversation just as smoothly as they had on email. It was as if they'd spoken on the phone all the time. Somehow the conversation moved to pets.

"I would love to have a dog, but I'm just not home enough," said Serenity.

"Do you like those cute little dogs I see women walking around with in their handbags?"

"Ha! I love those, but if I were to get a dog, I'd want a *big* one...a husky maybe. I'm one of those small girls that likes big things."

"Napoleon complex?" Chris willed his thoughts to focus on Serenity's words and not the innuendos her comment could have suggested. He chuckled. "Do you like big cars too?"

"Yes." Serenity giggled. "I drive an SUV. How'd you know?"

"Lucky guess."

"I need the space for the kids I work with. I carry loads of stuff in my car."

Relishing the soothing cadence of her voice, Chris kept the questions coming. It was then that he determined that her name was the perfect fit. He found the sound of her laughter even more titillating and leaned toward a more humorous slant, just to hear it flutter through the phone. Before he knew it, midnight arrived. They'd been talking for almost three hours. He yawned, which prompted him to look at his clock.

"Oh now, Chris. Don't yawn. It's—" he heard her yawn in her pause "—contagious!" She laughed. "Please excuse me."

"I didn't realize it was so late," he said, nestling into his lush pillow.

"Goodness! We've been on the phone forever. I can't believe it. I need to get to bed. I've got an early day tomorrow—actually, I've got early days every day."

"Me too. Can I call you tomorrow?"

"Sure. It's sweet that you asked." A comfortable silence expanded between them. "I guess I should be saying good-night."

"Yeah. Good night, Serenity. It was nice talking to you."

"Talk to you soon." She yawned again. "Excuse me. I'm sorry about that."

"No worries. I started it."

"You did." She giggled.

Despite their apparent fatigue, Chris wasn't ready to end the call and could tell that she wasn't either.

A few beats passed before she spoke again. "I'm glad we had this chance to talk."

"I am too."

Another moment passed. "Good night."

"Good night." Chris felt himself smile again.

Now that he had heard her voice, he wanted to see her face up close. He was intrigued.

# Chapter 9

"Don't you sound rather chipper today!"

Serenity stopped humming and spun on her heels to face Rayne. "Who, me?" She giggled.

"Yes, *you!* You're in here, singing. You've got all that bounce in your step." Rayne eyed her suspiciously. "What's going on?"

"What do you mean?" Serenity tried to keep a straight face, but her telling smile morphed into a full-on laugh. "I can't hide anything from you. Hold on." Serenity closed the door to the music room, went back to her desk and sat on the edge.

Rayne folded her arms, tilted her head and raised one brow.

"I met someone through the dating site."

Rayne's gasp was dramatic. "No! Is he cute? What does he do for a living? Where does he live? Did you go out already? How come you didn't tell me? Oh my goodness!" Rayne held her head in her hands. "Did you have sex?"

"Rayne!" Serenity yelled. "I haven't even seen him in person. Of course I didn't have sex with him."

Rayne closed her mouth abruptly. She looked like she could burst into a billion pieces. Serenity shook her head and laughed at Rayne, who tried to contain her own laughter by covering her mouth. Rayne's chuckles spilled right through her fingers.

"Okay." Rayne pressed her lips together and sat beside Serenity on her desk. "Tell me everything."

Serenity tilted her head. "Actually, there's not much to tell."

Rayne threw her head back and then gave her a sideways glance. "Then why all the glee?"

"I spoke to him for the first time last night." Serenity closed her eyes and shivered. "His voice was deep and so sexy."

"Uh…is this as juicy as it gets?" Rayne raised one brow.

"Ha! I know. So lame, but it was progress. We've been communicating only by email for a few weeks, and yesterday he asked for my number. I was hesitant at first. We ended up being on the phone for hours."

Rayne leaned closer to Serenity. "Okay. This seems to be getting better. What did you talk about?"

"Everything! Work, home, likes, dislikes, music and the fact that I like big things…" Serenity waited a moment for Rayne to catch on to the innuendo.

"Wait! What?" Understanding spread across Rayne's face and her mouth dropped. "You told him that?"

"Kind of." Serenity sunk into her shoulders and spread her lips into a toothy grin.

"Oh my goodness! What did he say?"

"He asked if I had a Napoleon complex." Serenity snickered.

Rayne shook her head. "Are you going to go out with him?"

Serenity slid off her desk and took a deep breath. "I want to, but I'm nervous. What if he's a lunatic?"

"And what if he's Mr. Right?" Rayne said, being direct. She hopped off the desk and stood in front of her friend. "Meet him at a coffeehouse or something. That way it's not too intimate, and there will be plenty of people there with you. Heck! Ethan and I can be there too. We'll swoop in and save you if things are not going well."

"That could work." Serenity contemplated.

"Tell him to meet you over at The Cozy Mug. Go early enough to get the big comfy chairs by the window. Ethan and I will get there early and sit nearby. He'll never suspect that we know you. Or maybe you should act surprised when you see us and he'll know not to mess with you. You'll be less likely to come up missing," she teased.

"That won't work. If he's that crazy, he'll be on his best behavior if he knows that other people I know are around. You'll have to act like strangers."

Serenity and Rayne looked at each other and hooted.

"We sound crazy, Rayne."

"Like we're seriously planning some covert operation."

"I'd never ask him out first anyway. If he suggests we meet, then I'll name the place. I'm an old-fashioned girl, remember."

Rayne rolled her eyes. "Whatever, Serenity. Old-fashioned girls miss out, waiting on boys to make the first move. Go for what you want, just like you do with those grants."

The bell rang. Instinctively, Serenity looked at her watch.

"I need to get to the third floor." Rayne trotted toward the music-room exit. "We'll finish this later."

The second bell rang, and the halls filled with teen

chatter. Serenity picked up her cell phone from the desk to place it in her purse. Before dropping it in, she tapped the home button to see if she had any notifications. Several red circles appeared, indicating how many alerts she had. She tapped the message icon and blushed at the brief text from Chris.

The message—a simple Hi, followed by it was great talking to you yesterday. I hope we can speak again soon—made her stomach flutter. Serenity wished she could go straight home after work and chat with him until she fell asleep again. He was so easy to talk to. It had been a long time since she'd enjoyed conversation with a man so much.

Serenity put her phone away and smiled at the students trickling into the class. This evening wouldn't work at all. She had to practice with the kids from her organization tonight. They had to be ready for their performance at the annual benefit in eight weeks. Most evenings wouldn't work, since she spent much of her time outside of school giving lessons, running the organization or managing her maid-of-honor duties. She took in a long deep breath and sighed. Once again she was reminded why the timing wasn't right for a relationship. Her plate was overflowing. It probably wouldn't even make sense to meet Chris in person.

She mustered some enthusiasm for her students and focused on being a music teacher for the next few periods. The end of the day approached quickly. She hadn't given much more thought to Chris or her phone. She fished the cell out of her bag as she walked toward the parking lot reserved for teachers. Hours had passed since she last checked it in class. Her screen was decorated with notifications.

Serenity checked her text messages first, hoping there

was something from Chris. He'd asked for a good time to call her later. She thumbed Nine o'clock and slipped the phone back into her bag.

Anticipating her conversation with Chris caused her to smile all through the rehearsals with her kids and all the way home from her studio slash office. By the time nine o'clock came, she was showered and had folded herself comfortably on the bed, flipping channels. She grinned when the phone rang and answered in a sultrier tone than she'd intended.

"Hey."

"Did you have a good day?" Chris's deep voice rumbled through the receiver.

He could say anything, Serenity thought, and it would sound sexy. "I did. Thanks," she answered. "What about you?"

This evening, the conversation was just as stimulating, volleying from travel to politics to favorite foods and embarrassing moments. They had so much in common. Serenity enjoyed their lively debates when their opinions separated into opposing views. His intelligence was a turn-on. During the long call, she sporadically laughed whenever she recalled his story about splitting his pants on an iron gate while on a triple date with his two best friends, their girlfriends and the girl he'd been crushing on for months. She could imagine the humiliation. He laughed just as hard when she told him about the only blind date she'd ever had, which started with her falling flat on her face as she stepped outside her front door.

Serenity lay on her side, listening to the deep timbre of Chris's voice. When he laughed, she felt the rumble in her chest and wondered what it would be like to meet him in person. All she'd seen were a few pictures and none of them were close up. Chris looked handsome enough in the photos, but her curiosity was growing. The more she found out about him, the more she wanted to know.

"Broadway shows or concerts?"

"What?" Chris said at first and then chuckled in recognition of the game. "Actually, both."

"You can only pick one."

"Concerts. What about you?"

"Both."

"That's not fair."

"You're right. As a music lover, I'd have to say concerts."

"I have one for you."

"Go for it."

"Chocolate or roses?"

"Definitely chocolate. Cut flowers remind me of funerals." Serenity grimaced as if he could see her face. Then she closed her eyes and enjoyed the sound of his laughter.

"Whew! I'm glad I asked."

Serenity's breath caught. Was he about to ask her out? She wasn't sure if she was ready. "Relaxing beach vacations or sightseeing excursions?" she asked quickly to deflect the inevitable.

"I would say I'm more of a traveler than a vacationer. I'd have to pick excursions. I like learning about other cultures."

"Me too." That answer sparked more conversations about places they wanted to visit. Greece was one they had in common.

Serenity nuzzled into her pillow and yawned. Her eyes grew heavy but she wasn't ready to end the conversation. She pushed on until she started nodding.

"It's almost one in the morning." Fatigue made Chris's voice sound hoarse.

"Goodness! I need to be up at six." Serenity groaned.

"I'll wake you up," he offered.

"You don't have to do that," she insisted.

"I'd love to hear your voice first thing in the morning."

Serenity cleared her throat. "I sound somewhat froggish. There's nothing attractive about it at all."

"Ha! I'm sure you still sound amazing."

Serenity's cheeks burned. He thought she sounded amazing.

"I'm up around the same time anyway. It won't be a problem."

"It's probably best. It will keep me from hitting the snooze button for an hour. I may have a better chance of getting to work on time." Serenity yawned again. "I'd better get to bed."

"I like talking to you."

"I like talking to you too."

Silence settled between them for a few moments. She sensed that he wanted to prolong the call as much as she did.

Serenity looked forward to starting her day with the sound of his voice. "Good night, Chris," she finally said.

Serenity fluffed her pillow, pulled the covers to her neck and closed her eyes with a smile on her lips. This was only their second time speaking on the phone, but she felt like she'd known him for some time. Now she yearned to see his face in person. His voice would resonate like a baritone serenade. Serenity hoped for a preview in her dreams.

# Chapter 10

*Good morning. Call me when you get a chance.*

Chris put his phone aside and leaned back onto the head-rest. He'd awakened with Serenity on his mind again. It was still early, but that was best. He planned to ask her to dinner. Hopefully she'd see his text and ring him soon. He smiled at the memory of their phone conversations this past week, which went on for hours at a time, just like the one last night. There was a familiar air when they spoke. He felt like he'd known her much longer. She was witty, intelligent and interesting, giving depth to their interactions. They eventually ventured into more flirtatious banter. There was a lot to like about Serenity, and he had yet to look into her eyes. Best of all, she didn't appear to be weird—so far. That's what he feared most with all this online dating. Based on what he found after checking into her, she seemed passionate and giving—two compelling traits that were missing in his dates of late.

Knowing so much about her almost seemed unfair, since she could only know things about him that he told her directly. He hadn't actually lied about anything except his name. He was careful never to mention the name of his family's business or the "restaurant" he "ran" with friends. He also never expected this online dating thing to yield any kind of viable results. Yet, something about Serenity pulled at him, even though he'd never met her in person. It had to happen soon. Chris needed to know what it was about her that compelled him.

This was an experiment. She'd already proven that there were decent girls online. Curiosity led their interactions. Now he wanted to explore more. Maybe after a few dates they would go their separate ways. Maybe he wouldn't need to tell Serenity who he really was. Or maybe...things would work out—surprising him and her. She'd mentioned her reservations about online dating too.

It was time to move beyond emails, texts and long talks on the phone. Serenity had begun to visit him in his dreams. He already imagined the feel of her skin, the scent of her hair and the unfiltered sound of that sweet voice of hers that reminded him of a sultry ballad.

Chris pushed the car door open and swung his legs over the step board, dismounting from the oversize SUV. Waving to several of Chandler Food Corp.'s employees as he walked, Chris headed through the parking lot toward the front door. Just as he reached for it, his phone rang. Quickly, he snatched it from the inside pocket of his suit jacket. He licked his lips instinctively when he saw Serenity's number and then chuckled when he realized what he'd done.

"Hello." His tone was collected. He turned from the door, stepping aside as other employees made their way inside.

"Good morning," Serenity sang.

Chris walked away from the entrance. "Good morning yourself. Are you tired?" Asking the question reminded him of how little sleep he had had in the past week. They'd spoken every single night. An involuntary yawn followed. Chris shook his head.

"I'm exhausted! Luckily my students keep me alert." She paused for a moment. "I got your text."

"Yes." Chris remembered. Hearing her voice was a pleasure that made him forget things at times. He chuckled. "I was wondering if you were busy tonight."

"Oh…" Several beats passed.

Maybe she wasn't ready for this, Chris thought. He wasn't letting up, though.

"You still there?"

"I'm sorry." Serenity released a nervous laugh. "I'm giving a lesson tonight. I'll be finished around seven o'clock. Why?"

"I'd like to take you to dinner." Chris heard her clear her throat. He'd come to notice she did that when she wanted to take her time answering a question. "Do you have a favorite place?"

The purpose of his question was twofold. One, it was important to him that she feel comfortable and, two, he didn't want to go anywhere that he usually frequented. As vast as Long Island was, it was a small community. There were only a few degrees of separation. Everyone knew someone who knew of someone within the circles in which he operated. Chris would be less likely to run into anyone he knew on her side of town. His research showed that he and Serenity lived on opposite ends of the island. His family was spread across the far north, bordering the wealth of the Long Island Sound, and she hailed from the South Shore.

"Have I not done enough to convince you that I'm not crazy?"

Serenity's laugh floated through the phone like a pleasant melody. Chris was happy to lighten the air between them, dispersing the tension that followed his inquiry.

"How do you know that I'm not the crazy one?" Serenity feigned an evil laugh.

"My insanity detectors are highly sensitive. We wouldn't have gotten past the first few emails, let alone the second phone call. I'm convinced that you're pretty sane. If not, I'll find out for sure if you allow me the pleasure of taking you to dinner tonight."

"How about we start with coffee?"

"That's cool with me."

"Have you ever been to The Cozy Mug?"

"Nice name, but no. So it's a date?"

"It's a date."

Chris closed his free hand and gave a small fist pump. "Great. Does seven thirty work for you?"

"Perfectly."

"Good. I need to get into work. Call you later?"

"Sure. I'll text the address."

"Thanks. And next time, I get to pick the place."

"Hmm. You sound pretty confident about there being a next time."

"I'm a confident kind of guy." Serenity chuckled, and again it reminded him of music. "Good day to you, Ms. Williams."

"And you as well, Mr. Mullins."

He almost asked who Mr. Mullins was and caught himself.

Once the call ended, Chris entered Chandler Food Corp.'s headquarters. A smile that generated from somewhere in his core shined on his face. Several employees greeted him with inquisitive smiles.

He was just starting his day but already felt accomplished. He'd worn one of his favorite suits and driven the SUV in anticipation of seeing Serenity that evening. He remembered her saying that she liked big things. His Escalade was far larger than the Porsche and potentially less pretentious. His self-assurance was intact. He hadn't expected her to decline. She was curious just like him.

Ideas of how things would turn out later visited him throughout the day. Would Serenity be like the woman who had been appearing in his dreams recently? Would their conversation flow as easily in person as on the phone? He was sure she'd be just as beautiful as she was in her pictures, if not more. Would he see anyone who knew him? Most people called him Chris anyway, so even if he did run into someone, he could manage the interaction and avoid revealing too much.

Chris returned from his third meeting since the morning. There had been only one on his calendar, but a crisis had yanked him from his planned schedule and demanded his time and attention. Mentally worn out, he plopped in his chair and closed his eyes, relieved that the day was almost over.

"Can you believe this mess?"

Chris opened his eyes to see his sister Jewel marching into his office with one hand on her hip. She parked herself in front of his desk and huffed. She sat hard and then lifted both hands to massage her temples.

"It's the economy, sis."

"Which I thought was getting better!"

"It will work out."

"How? The entire supermarket chain is folding. That's a huge chunk of business for us."

"Those stores can't stay empty long. There's a new chain that's planning to open fifty locations across Westchester and Long Island. I've already met with their investors."

"That's going to take months. What do we do in the meantime?" Jewel sat up. "We're going to feel this loss for a few months." She flopped back in the chair.

Chris knew this to be true. He stood and headed to the window overlooking the walking path that snaked around a large fountain and rose over a koi pond by a footbridge—a welcome addition from the last renovation the company had made to its grounds. Stuffing his hands in his pockets, he sighed.

A moment later, Chris turned abruptly, hurried back to his desk and flipped through folders in search of notes. "Here it is."

"What's that?" Jewel stood and walked to Chris's side of the desk to view the papers he held in his hand.

"There's a small chain of boutique markets that are opening up a few stores in our area. They're one of those places that only sell organic foods. The first store is set to open this summer. I'll have my team check into their progress and see if they're on track to start their grand openings. I'm sure we can get our gluten-free and organic fruit pies in there. That will fill some of the gap."

Jewel sighed. "It's a start, but I still won't come in on target based on our projections from the end of the year. You know I hate it when I don't make my numbers."

"Your numbers are my numbers. We will make it."

Jewel smiled. "I love how collected you seem to be in the midst of crisis. I can learn from you, little bro."

"'Cause I'm smarter."

Jewel swatted him on the head. Chris ducked but got hit anyway.

"Seriously. We'll get through this." He touched her nose.

"We have to," Jewel said, still sounding dejected. "Dad

charged us with coming up with a strategy to minimize our losses." She turned to her brother. "We can start tonight. Come by. I'll make dinner."

"Whoa! First of all, I want to make it to see tomorrow. No need for you to go anywhere near the kitchen. Besides, I have plans for tonight."

"Boy! You know I can cook." Jewel folded her arms in front of her and twisted her lips at him.

Chris chuckled.

"And where are you going? You don't have to be at The Reserve tonight?"

"I have other plans."

Jewel tilted her head and eyed him through narrow slits. "A new one. What's her name? As a matter of fact, forget it. You don't keep them around long enough for me to learn any names. Have fun. We'll get started on the strategic plan tomorrow."

"What's that supposed to mean?" Chris asked Jewel's retreating back.

Jewel waved over her shoulder, dismissing his inquiry as she walked out his office. Chris knew what she'd meant. It had been years since he introduced someone to his sisters who didn't disappear after a few short weeks. Serenity didn't even know his real name. There was no telling how long she'd be around—even though he liked her without really knowing her yet. Tonight that could change.

# Chapter 11

Serenity could never have anticipated the events of her day. Cutbacks led to one of the music teachers being laid off, and Serenity had to pick up two more classes plus work with the show choir. That left her with only one free period besides lunch. Time management would become more challenging than it had ever been.

This also meant more time had to be dedicated to prepping for the additional classes, limiting the time she had to work on Rayne's wedding and Heartstrings. She and Elisa had a bridal shower to plan and a bride-to-be to keep calm. For Heartstrings, there were grant proposals that had to be written and submitted, lessons to be given, recitals to rehearse for and a gala to plan. She and Rayne were the only two actual employees. Volunteers often helped with programs and lessons, but only at their convenience. Their board members were helpful but not musically inclined or grant-savvy. Serenity would have to let them know that she'd need more of their support for planning the gala. That, she knew, they'd be capable of handling.

What worried her the most was the grant proposal

they were due to submit in a few days. If funded, Serenity would be able to take her mission abroad, as part of a program to bring the arts and instruments to kids in a poverty-stricken community in South America. She planned to take a leave of absence to run the program herself. But now that her school was down a music teacher and she'd been given the bulk of the work, how could she ask for that leave of absence for an entire school year?

The stress of all this sudden work made her want to cancel both her lessons and her date with Chris at the coffee shop. She was tired but determined to make it through. Working with her kids from the organization always made her spirit dance, and she'd waited long enough to meet Chris in person.

She opened the first closet in the music room, where she kept her belongings and had hung a mirror. Turning from side to side, she realized she looked as weary as she felt. The vibrant pink lipstick had all but disappeared, leaving only traces in the crevices of her plump lips. Eyeliner had smudged under her eyes, partly from the tears she'd shed, saying goodbye to her fellow music teacher. Serenity retrieved a few wipes from the box she kept for her students and analyzed her reflection once more before wiping the spotty makeup from her face. The cool moist cloth soothed her skin, dabbing away some of the stress of her day. She poured a dime-sized amount of cream on her hand and massaged it into her face. Then she refreshed her eyeliner and mascara and painted on a new coat of lipstick.

Checking her reflection once more, she realized she still looked a little tired, but it was the best she could do. At least her resemblance to a raccoon was gone. Somehow she would manage.

She arrived at the community center a few minutes

early. Most of the students she worked with were already there. Beginning the lesson right away gave her less time to think about all the changes that had transpired at school. Before she knew it, seven o'clock had come. She had hoped to leave a few minutes early.

"Okay, guys. Circle up."

The kids obliged, putting away their instruments, lining them up neatly by the door and taking hold of one another's hands.

"Lauren, would you like to lead tonight?" Serenity asked a quiet, heavyset young lady.

"Sure, Ms. Serenity." The girl cleared her throat. Serenity smiled, cherishing her willingness to always lead. "I am talented," she declared. The rest of the group repeated what she said. "I am important." Once again, the group responded with the same words. "I am enough!" The enthusiasm that Lauren used to proclaim the last line of their ritual made Serenity's heart swell.

"I am enough!" the group yelled.

"See you next week, everyone. Don't forget to practice. We only have a few weeks left before the gala."

"Yes, Ms. Serenity," several of them yelled in unison.

Twin girls ran to her and wrapped their arms around her waist. She squeezed them tight.

"Ms. Serenity." One of the twins released her and pulled out her cell phone. "Can you teach us how to play this?" The young girl tapped her way to YouTube. "This guy is lit," she said in teen language describing how good they thought the musician was.

"Let me see if he's as good as you claim," Serenity said.

"I'm serious. He plays Champagne's new song on the violin. You have to see this." The girls played the artist's video.

"Isn't he so good, Ms. Serenity?"

"And he's cute too," the twin sister said. The girls snickered. Serenity raised her brow and their snickers turned to full-on laughter.

Acclaimed violinist Storm Kensington played a beautiful upbeat version of the R&B artist's latest release. Serenity and the girls bobbed their heads to the beat. Serenity was excited that the girls were so intrigued by an artist she also admired and his incredible ability to freestyle popular music.

"Wasn't he great?"

"Yes he was, girls."

"See, I told you he was lit."

Serenity laughed. "It looks like your mom is here."

"Bye, Ms. Serenity." The girls walked off, giggling about how cute Storm looked in the video.

For a fleeting moment, Serenity thought it would be cool to have someone like him visit the kids and play for them. Just as quickly as the thought came, she shook it off. How would she get a celebrity of that caliber to come to visit her program?

Serenity looked at her watch. It was now ten after seven. "Shoot!" With the frenzy of the day, she had forgotten to tell Rayne she was meeting Chris at the coffee shop. She wanted Rayne and Ethan to be there.

On the way to her car, Serenity called Chris and asked if they could push the time back to eight o'clock. That would give her time to speak with Rayne and stop by her house to freshen up. The coffee shop was only ten minutes from her house. Serenity reached out to Rayne after she finished speaking with Chris.

"Of course we'll come. We'll get there before you arrive."

"Yes!" Serenity shrieked. "Thank you so much."

"I can't wait to see him. He looks like a real cutie from the pictures you showed me."

"I can't wait either." Serenity pulled up in front of her apartment. "I'm home. I'll call you when I'm on my way."

Serenity washed her face, brushed her teeth and refreshed her makeup in about ten minutes. Without much more time to spare, she changed her shoes, slipping into a pair of heels. The sleek style added height to her petite frame and gave her a more chic appeal than the flat riding boots she changed from.

She trotted back to the car, turned the key in the ignition, but sat still for a moment before driving off.

"I can't believe I'm doing this," she said to the rearview mirror. Three deep breaths calmed her breathing. She wasn't backing out now.

Tapping out a quick text to Rayne, she sighed. Rayne replied right away, letting her know that she had arrived. Serenity shifted the car into gear, closed her eyes briefly and swallowed hard before pulling off.

The ten-minute drive proved nerve-racking. Serenity swore she'd caught every possible light and each stayed red a minute longer just because she was anxious. Luckily she pulled right into a spot that someone was leaving as she drove up. She turned the key, shut off the ignition and sat back another moment. Peering through the window, she tried to see if she could recognize Chris but couldn't get a good enough view of everyone inside the dimly lit coffee bar.

"Let's do this, girl." She pushed the door open and took one step at a time despite her beating heart.

She spotted Rayne and Ethan sitting at table near the window as soon as she walked in. Rayne discreetly winked but gave no other indication that she knew Serenity.

Then she saw him. Her breath caught. He tilted his head in a familiar way. Serenity smiled, confirming the inquiry in his expression. He stood, lifting into his full, grand height. She guessed he was over six feet, nearly a foot above her height. She assessed him as he made his way over to her—smooth skin, piercing eyes, and a tight-set jaw. His friendly grin revealed a cavernous set of dimples. In that instant, he was even better-looking. She wondered if his shirt and slacks knew how blessed they were to cover such an amazing body.

Chris's pictures couldn't possibly have lived up to the task of doing him justice.

"Serenity?" His voice flowed from his mouth and rumbled her core like the strum of a bass guitar.

Serenity thought her knees would waver. She cleared her throat. "Pleasure to meet you—" she cleared her throat "—Chris."

Chris took her hand and kissed the back of it. "Likewise." He licked those scrumptious lips and Serenity felt something flutter inside her belly. "What are you having?"

Without releasing her hand, he walked over to the counter.

"Chai… I'll have a chai tea latte. That's my favorite."

Chris placed their orders, and they stepped aside to wait.

"You look even better in person."

Serenity felt her cheeks burn. "You don't look so bad yourself."

Chris chuckled. "Thanks."

They engaged in small talk until the barista called their names. Taking her by the hand once more, Chris led her back to the spot where he'd been sitting. It was the exact spot that Rayne had suggested, with the cozy oversize chairs and a small accent table between them. Chris waited for her to sit before he did.

"We're finally here—together."

"I know." Serenity couldn't help her smile. "It seems strange. I feel like I've known you forever, yet this is the first time I've seen you."

"Yeah. I know. It does feel strange. Tell me more about Heartstrings."

Nothing made Serenity happier. Her last boyfriend considered her service a waste of time and never encouraged her to pursue it as a business. Serenity filled Chris in on everything she loved about the organization—the kids, the board, their supporters. She shared her earlier encounter with the twins and expressed the fact that she wished she could get more professional musicians or celebrities involved with the organization.

Chris talked about his new venture with his friends and how much fun it was to work with them. Lost in conversation, time passed and Serenity barely noticed. She'd grown completely comfortable in his presence. They'd entered that familiar space again. The same one they'd created first on email and then by phone, cocooned by their intrigue for one another. No subject went undiscovered. They debated, laughed, flirted and drank each other in. He held her in intense gazes for moments at a time, making her blush. She got lost in those beautiful brown orbs, floating on the promise of future pleasures.

Being in public didn't matter. It was just the two of them in that coffeehouse until it was truly only Serenity, Chris, Rayne and Ethan. Serenity's phone buzzed. Rayne sent a message asking if she needed them to stick around any longer. She replied yes and promised to end their rendezvous within minutes.

"I hate to, but I really need to head home. I have some additional prep to do for my classes tomorrow."

Chris looked at his watch, then looked around the coffeehouse. "I guess it is time to go. We seem to be the only ones left besides that other couple." He smiled, and Serenity thought she felt her heart melting.

Serenity just smiled.

"Let me walk you to your car."

"Okay."

Chris helped her to her feet. Taking her hand, he led her past Rayne and Ethan and escorted her to her car parked right out front. Serenity pressed the key fob, unlocking the doors with a chirp. Chris opened her door and stepped aside. Serenity stood by the open door, looked up at him and then down. She didn't want this to end.

"Good night, Chris."

His smile warmed her on the inside. His voice dipped. His eyes lowered to a sexy gaze. "Good night."

For several minutes neither of them spoke. They stood with their eyes locked on one another.

"Good night, Chris," she said again.

"Good night." Chris leaned forward and kissed her cheek.

Serenity felt her skin tingle at the place where he'd pressed his lips against her face.

"I hope that now you will allow me to take you to dinner."

"I think that could work." Serenity pretended to ponder the idea.

Chris shook his head, chuckling. "Call me when you get in."

"Will do."

Slowly he stepped back and closed her door. He stood for another moment before waving goodbye and heading to his car. Serenity sat in her car a few moments longer, willing her heartbeat to return to a normal pace.

Her phone buzzed.

Rayne sent a single word text. Whoa!

Serenity dialed her number.

"Girl!" Rayne sang into the phone, and the two of them laughed. "Ethan said he's glad he didn't have to bust out with some of his mixed martial arts moves on that guy. He seemed cool."

"Tell my buddy I said thanks for having my back."

"All right! I'll see you tomorrow at work. We're exhausted. You two sure can talk."

"I know. Thanks again. Let me know that you got home safe."

"Okay. Nighty-night."

Minutes later, Serenity was in front of her apartment complex. She barely remembered driving home. Every thought was a reflection of the time she'd just spent with Chris. She definitely wanted to see him again.

Serenity strolled into her apartment with a smile parting her lips and dropped her bag on the table near the door. A single note alerted her to the incoming text. Serenity picked up the phone, hoping it was from Chris. It was. Her smile broadened.

Home safe?

Yes. She couldn't help but chuckle. The attention Chris lavished her with had her feeling giddy.

Good. Can I take you to dinner Friday?

I'd love that.

Without chaperones this time?

"What?" Serenity said aloud. One hand flew to her gaping mouth before she responded.

How'd you know?

Ha! Their constant staring didn't alarm you.

Busted!! Serenity entered three laughing emojis. No chaperones this time. I promise.

Looking forward to it.

Me too.

Good night.

Good night.

Cradling her phone in both hands, she held it to her chest and closed her eyes. Friday couldn't come soon enough.

## Chapter 12

"So when do we meet her, Chris?" From the tone of Jewel's voice, Chris could picture her standing with her arms firmly folded in front of her as she tapped one foot.

"Who knows?"

"Pfft! You wouldn't spend so much brainpower on planning a nice date if she was just any ole woman. This one is special, whether you want to admit it or not," Jade summed. "What does she look like? Is she stunning?"

"Thanks for the ideas. I'm getting off the phone now. I need to get ready for my date, remember?"

"Chris." Jade groaned.

"Love y'all. Bye." Chris ended the call before they could protest any further. He was done with their interrogation but thankful for what they had helped him plan.

Taking special care with his preparation, he checked in with Serenity and confirmed his arrangements. Several times, he questioned his desire to put so much effort into planning this first official date. How far could they really go, when he hadn't revealed his true identity?

Chris decided to use this date as a gauge to determine

whether or not this relationship had real potential. If not, there would be no need to tell Serenity who he was.

"Ha!" Chris laughed at himself. Who was he fooling?

His sisters were right. There was something about this woman. The way Serenity and he glided into easy banter, the comfort they felt in each other's presence—all of that intrigued him. He hadn't spent hours on the phone with a woman since his teen crush. There was never a dull moment with Serenity. No lulls in their conversation. Every bout of silence was cozy and companionable, connecting stimulating deliberations like hyphens.

When he had finally seen her in person, he'd been taken aback. A stunning beauty packed into a petite frame made her presence grandiose. Immediately he'd wanted to run his fingers through the unruly coils in her hair, which framed a striking face, sharp cheekbones and large brown eyes that threatened to weaken his sensibilities. He'd wanted to kiss those full sweetheart lips the second he'd greeted her in the coffee shop. The pictures he'd seen on her social media profiles failed to replicate her raw beauty.

Chris had forced himself to peel his attention away from her eyes. That's when he'd discovered her curves. Ample mounds created perfect arcs under her cashmere sweater. His father would have said she had the shape of a Coca-Cola bottle. She was everything he'd envisioned and more. It seemed unreal, almost unfair, to house such beauty, wit, intelligence and passion in a compact existence.

Standing before the full-length mirror in his bedroom, he tugged at his blazer, straightening it at the hem. He adjusted the collar of his stark-white shirt. The jeans and stylish shoes finished the look with a casual but refined flair.

Assessing his attire, Chris wondered how he would explain his reason for the fake name if and when the time came. "Eh." Waving off those concerns, he grabbed the keys to his SUV. His intentions weren't to be deceptive. He just wanted to find someone who wasn't driven to him by his legacy. Surely, she'd understand that.

He rolled up to her apartment complex, which was nestled between middle-class houses, at exactly six thirty as he'd promised. Her cozy, tree-lined neighborhood felt welcoming and reminded him of his grandparents' home. Children whizzed past on bikes. Professionals hurried home from work. Parents rushed kids into minivans, slamming doors and complaining of being late to practices. People walked mild-mannered pets that appeared unaffected by the lively buzz of the community. Her neighborhood was so different than his. There weren't any equestrian centers or sprawling estates set widely apart from the next. Kids didn't play in his streets. They released their recreational energies in acres of pool houses, or at country clubs, practices or lessons, and spread their cultural wings abroad.

Immediately, Chris appreciated the simplicity that seemed to adorn the lifestyle this neighborhood exemplified. He was certain that these cool people didn't pursue pedigrees and legacies with the same fervor as those in his circle.

Chris felt a few eyes on him as he made it up the walkway to Serenity's front door. She opened it after a few taps, inviting him in as she slid an earring through her ear.

"Good evening." Chris leaned forward, planting a kiss on her cheek. A delicate floral scent wafted into his nostrils. He breathed it in.

"Good evening to you." Serenity received his hug. "Can I get you anything?"

"I'm fine. Thanks."

"Okay. I just need to get my shoes, and I'll be ready." She disappeared down the hall.

Chris took in the eclectic composition of her home. Her decor was a direct reflection of her nature—composed, artistic and stylish. She paired antique furnishings, full of character, with sleek modern accents, and plush seating filled with colorful throws and inviting pillows. Every piece in the room was interesting and meticulously placed. An older piano sat proudly in a corner by the window. It was clear that Serenity surrounded herself with things that she loved—music, art and children. He recognized her in pictures with students and people he assumed were family members because of their shared features.

"Ready!" Serenity appeared, startling Chris.

"You have a beautiful home."

"Thanks! It's my sanctuary. Shall we go?"

Her home enveloped him. Chris wanted to stay a little longer but remembered his plans. "Let's go." Like a gentleman, Chris led her to the car and made sure she was settled in before taking the driver's seat.

The ride to Manhattan seemed short with the flow of conversation between them.

"Where did you say we were going?" Serenity asked.

"I didn't," he said, eyeing her. "You'll see soon enough."

"I hate surprises. Ha! I'm a liar. I absolutely love them. I think it says a lot about a person when they go through the trouble of planning surprises. You can't help but feel special that someone went through so much for you."

"That's good to know."

"Are you taking notes on me?"

"Uh. Yep."

Serenity's head fell back as she laughed. Chris took in the lines of her neck and shoulders and wondered how smooth her skin must feel there.

"Very interesting, Mr. Mullins."

Chris cleared his throat. That was the third time she'd called him that. This time it felt more foreign than before.

"Mr. Mullins is way too formal." He forced a chuckle.

Serenity laughed. "We're here already?" she asked as Chris pulled into a parking garage.

"Ready for a good time?"

"Yes!" Her titter sounded like music.

Chris gave the keys to an attendant, took Serenity's hand and led her down the bustling Manhattan Street.

"No way!" she said and looked at Chris as they walked up to the concert hall known for hosting the nation's most renowned jazz artists.

"Surprise!"

Serenity shrieked, covered her mouth and looked up at the sign. "We're going to see Storm Kensington! Oh my goodness! I can't believe this." Serenity wrapped her arms around Chris. "This is an amazing surprise."

Chris felt his ego swell a bit. He wanted to say, "Wait until the rest of the evening" but bit back that comment. Her response now was priceless, and he looked forward to seeing it again.

Inside, an usher escorted them to front-row seats. Serenity sat on the edge of her seat for the entire concert, getting lost in the rhythms. Chris watched her dance and sway—eyes closed as she felt the music. It seemed to flow through her. At the end, he swore she clapped the loudest.

"That was fantastic! Thank you so much, Chris."

"We need to hurry." Chris took her hand. Serenity

looked puzzled but gathered her scarf. "We've been invited backstage."

"Wait! What?" Serenity rolled her eyes upward and slumped back down into the chair, pretending to faint. Opening one eye, she looked up at Chris. "You can't be serious."

"You're a character."

"This is too much. I can't believe we're going backstage to meet Storm Kensington. I wish my students were here to see this. They'd lose their minds."

Hand in hand, they headed backstage. Storm was sweaty but polite as he greeted Serenity and Chris. She praised his performance and told him how much the kids she worked with at the community center loved him.

"I'd love to come by and meet them," Storm offered.

Serenity's mouth dropped. She looked at Chris and then at Storm. They looked at each other and laughed.

"You would?" Serenity was in awe.

Chris felt the swell of pride again.

"For sure! Here." Storm dug in a duffel bag, retrieved a card and handed it to her. "Shoot me an email, and we can figure out some dates when I'm back in town."

"Thank you so much. My kids will be amazed." Serenity hugged Storm.

Storm gave Chris a firm handshake. "Pleasure, my man."

"Thank you," Chris replied. "The pleasure was ours."

"And I'll see you soon." He shook Serenity's hand.

"Looking forward to it." She smiled.

Chris turned to her. "Ready to eat?"

"Oh, yes. I'm starving."

"Let's go."

Chris retrieved the car and headed uptown. Serenity spoke mostly of how excited her students were going to be to meet Storm. She decided to let it be a surprise. Minutes later, Chris pulled up in front of the Jazz Museum. Serenity had been so engrossed in talking about her students, she didn't realize where they were until he took her by the hand and helped her out of the car.

"Surprise number two!"

"Is this the Jazz Museum? I thought we were going to eat. I've been meaning to come here. I want to schedule a trip here for the students at my school."

Chris just smiled.

"Wait." Serenity looked at her phone. "It's almost ten o'clock. Shouldn't it be closed?"

Chris placed a finger on her lips, quieting her. "Don't worry about that." Chris continued to the entrance, knocked and the door opened immediately.

A gangly gentleman shook Chris's hand and led them through the museum to a large gallery. In the center was a table set for two in crisp white linen, topped with flowers in a slim vase and a bowl of small floating candles. Low lighting cast an amber glow throughout the space. Jazz music flowed through hidden speakers.

"Would you prefer your personal tour before or after our meal?"

Serenity shook her head, beaming with appreciation. "Before would be nice."

Together they went from room to room, reading about jazz greats and the well-known history of jazz music in Harlem. When they returned, salads had been placed on the table.

Chris pulled Serenity's chair out before sitting.

"I know I keep saying it, but this is amazing. Thank you."

"You're welcome."

As usual, conversation came unhindered. They broached the subject of exes.

"We wanted different things and realized it was best to part ways," said Chris.

"What were the differences?" Serenity pricked a fingerling potato with her fork.

He was careful not to reveal too much. "She pictured a life very different from what I'd imagined. When we broke up, she got married months later, but it didn't last a year."

"Wow. That's unfortunate."

"And you?"

"My ex was a habitual liar. You wouldn't believe how many lies I caught him in. I never understood why he felt compelled. It really bothered me because it reminded me of my dad—" She sat up straight, tucking her lips. "I'm sorry. I'm saying too much."

"It's okay."

She huffed and placed her fork on the edge of her plate. "My stepdad raised me. My biological dad wasn't the best example of a father. He promised to marry my mom. She got pregnant, had me, and he still didn't marry her. He would always promise to take me places or spend time with me, and it never happened. Then one day, we found out why. He was already married and had a family on the other side of town."

"How old were you?"

"I was five, and I remember like it was yesterday. My mother was so angry she broke every window in his car. After that, I didn't see him for months. I hate liars." Serenity pushed the food around on her plate for a moment. "When I realized my ex was like my father, I ended it and haven't looked back."

Chris remained quiet for a moment. "How's your food?"

Serenity sat back. "I'm sorry. I didn't mean to spoil the mood. The food is delicious, and I'm having a wonderful time. Let's talk about something else."

"Yes. Let's do that," Chris said.

# Chapter 13

Chris became quiet. The two sat at the dinner table with the most silence they'd ever experienced. She continued to push her food around the plate, took a small bite of her sea bass and put the fork down. She hadn't meant to sully the atmosphere.

"How's your meal?" she asked, finally breaking the silence.

"It's great! Yours?"

Serenity took a long breath. "I think we now know enough about our exes to never bring the subject up again. Cool?"

Chris's sexy smile caused a shiver to squiggle down her back. "Cool."

"Tell me." Serenity paused, momentarily taken by his piercing brown eyes. She cleared her throat and picked up a piece of asparagus. "How'd you manage to make this happen?" she asked, waving her fork around. "The concert, backstage and this beautiful museum."

"I have friends."

Chewing slowly, Serenity gave him a sideways glance. "Friends, huh?"

"Yep." Chris picked up his wineglass and smiled over the rim. "Good friends."

"In high places, I assume." She shrugged. "It doesn't matter. This is wonderful. I need to make it up to you."

"That's not necessary." Chris took the napkin from his lap and placed it on the table. She sat back, looking completely sated.

"I know, but I still want to." She thought for a moment. "How about I cook dinner for you? I'm a great cook. Are you busy tomorrow?"

Chris groaned. "Unfortunately I am."

"Oh!" Serenity averted her eyes and then cleared her throat once again. She wondered if she was pushing it and was almost surprised at herself for taking such a lead. Professionally, she went after what she wanted. With men, she was more laid back. It was her old-fashioned way.

"How about Sunday?"

Serenity sniffed out a small chuckle at her brief bout of insecurity. "Actually, Sunday works fine."

"I'm a great cook too, you know."

"Really." Serenity released the word slowly, before sipping her wine. "Who taught you?"

"My mother, father and grandparents. They're all great cooks."

"That's so cool. What's your best dish?"

Chris sat back, his eyes narrowed and shifted toward the ceiling as he rubbed his leg pensively. "I make an awesome chili, and my pecan pie—" Chris kissed the gathered tips of his fingers "—to die for!"

"Seriously?"

Chris nodded modestly.

"I absolutely love pecan pie. My grandmother made the best I'd ever tasted."

"You haven't tasted mine."

"You can't compete with my nana." She swatted her hand in his direction. "Other than hers, the only one I found to be almost as good is the Mary Kate pies they sell in the supermarkets. I love those." Serenity closed her eyes and drew her shoulders in. "Now that my nana's gone, that's how I get my fix. My mother never perfected the recipe, so she doesn't make them. I wish I learned from Nana." She shook her head.

Serenity reminisced for a moment.

"I can teach you," Chris offered. "I'll bring the ingredients with me on Sunday."

Serenity gasped. "That would be awesome! I haven't had a homemade pecan pie in years."

"Let me warn you. You just might like it better than your grandmother's."

"No way, buddy." Serenity wagged her finger. "Nobody's pie beats Nana's."

"We'll see on Sunday." Chris raised one brow.

"I accept that challenge." Serenity held up her wineglass. Chris raised his and connected with a clink.

The familiar flow of their conversations returned. Serenity felt comfortable again. Chris drove her to his favorite wine bar in Manhattan and shared a few glasses of Cabernet with dessert, before heading back to Long Island.

Before going out with Chris, Serenity hadn't been on a real date in over a year. The evening out with him broke the cycle in a major way. No man had ever put that much thought into taking her out. Dinner, plays, movies and lounges had been the routine. Tonight, Chris indulged her passion for music and the arts in the most romantic way. He was thoughtful, considerate and attentive, and that winning mix had her intrigued.

When he pulled up in front of her complex, she thought of a way to keep the night going. Normally, she wouldn't invite a man into her home at the end of their first date. She didn't count their meeting at the coffeehouse as an actual date. It had been more like an informational interview. Tonight was a different story. She'd anticipated kissing his full lips from the moment he picked her up. She already knew that when their lips touched, it would be divinely explosive.

She watched him with anxious anticipation as he walked around the car to her passenger door. Opening it, he held out his hand. She took it, and her pulse quickened. Serenity wondered if he could somehow tell. Placing one heeled foot out of the car, she looked up at Chris. That sexy smile of his made her giggle. He held her steady as her second foot hit the pavement. She stood but tripped forward and landed right against his chest. Her breath caught, and a shiver ran down her spine. Instead of being embarrassed, she felt aware of her femininity cradled by his frame. She liked it there.

"Oops."

"I've got you." Chris's voice lowered. The husky tone was drowned in seduction.

For a moment neither of them moved. Chris wrapped his arms around her body. She could have lived right there.

"Mmm." She moaned, nestling against him.

Serenity closed her eyes for a moment. She felt Chris's hands run through her hair. She moaned again. With her head nestled in his chest, she could feel his heart rate quicken. Hers followed suit. Then her core clenched. Desire rolled over her in a slow, hot wave.

Chris released his embrace and cupped her face in his hands. Sparks of yearning shot through her. He studied her eyes at first. She matched his gaze. Chris drew closer. Serenity braced herself. Instinctively, her lips parted. Chris gently pressed his mouth against hers. She received him eagerly. Their tongues entwined in a heated and sultry dance. He devoured her, melting away every reservation. They parted long enough to catch their breath and continued kissing. Their passion threatened to set them ablaze. He kissed her more deeply. Her knees nearly buckled.

Serenity needed to catch her breath again but couldn't pull away. Chris was absolutely delicious to her, making her desire more of him. She squeezed him tighter. He pulled her in, pressing her body snugly against his. She felt his abs harden. His manhood flinched.

Chris let her go abruptly. Panting, his eyes remained closed. He needed to get himself together, it seemed. Serenity's chest heaved. Her entire body felt feverish. Dropping her head back, she sighed. A moan escaped. They'd reached an erotic edge. Only a fast break would keep them from going over.

When Serenity opened her eyes, Chris was staring at her. Desire flashed in his beautiful, brown orbs. He laced his fingers between hers and leaned forward again. Slow, sweet pecks led into another long passionate kiss.

Serenity was about to invite him inside but remembered this was just their first date. She had never felt so familiar with a man so soon.

"I need…"

"I should go now."

"Yes…" Serenity swallowed. She didn't really want him to go. "You should."

They never left the side of the car. Chris stepped back giving her space.

"I have to walk you to your door," he insisted.

"Okay." Serenity tugged on her shirt, straightening it, and looked around the parking lot. They hadn't thought about anyone seeing them until now. Blinded by desire, she'd received him greedily, without thinking. She hoped they weren't a spectacle. A part of her didn't care. He held her hand. She still tingled from his earlier touch.

At her door, he saw her in. After one quick controlled kiss, he left. Serenity watched him through the window until she could no longer see him. Then she turned and pressed her back against the wall. She shut her eyes and willed the heat ravaging her body to cool down and release her.

Sunday was a day away. She had invited him to her house for dinner, and he had accepted. She wondered if she'd be able to control her urges when he returned.

## Chapter 14

He had to tell her the truth. But how?

Chris pulled into the guest parking spot near Serenity's apartment. Friday night's date both enticed and haunted him. He had thoroughly enjoyed her company, relished her delight when she'd reacted so excitedly to his surprises, and almost exploded when they shared that passionate kiss by the car. Yet her distaste for lying men plagued him. He wasn't a liar. He had his reason for what he'd done, and his intent wasn't deception. However, he never expected to be here, wanting more, wanting to see where this thing with Serenity and him could go, and instinctively knowing it could go all the way.

He had needed to get past that first date to know if it made sense to go forward. Now he knew for sure that he wanted to continue seeing her. He'd tell her today. Before, during or after dinner, he wasn't sure. The timing had to be right. Once he explained himself, she'd understand his need for discretion.

He laughed, hard. Despite feeling like he'd know her forever, it had been less than a week since he'd seen her for the first time. How had he become so smitten so soon? His friends would surely tease him about this.

Huffing, he cut off the engine, grabbed the bag with the ingredients for the pie and got out of the car. He'd tell her today. No matter what. His decision was made by the time he reached the door.

Chris had only halfway pressed the bell when the door swung open. The sight of Serenity and her beautiful smile threatened to take his breath away. That had never happened before. Her hair was piled in a disorderly bun at the top of her head, giving her a bit of the "after sex" look and making her incredibly desirable. Under her frilly apron, her long sweater exposed one shoulder, revealing smooth, delectable skin. Leggings covered curves and toned legs like another layer of skin. He fought the urge to kiss the dip between her neck and shoulder. Bare feet showcased perfect toes polished with glitter. Her cozy appearance showed how naturally beautiful she was and made him want to lift her off her feet and carry her away.

"Hey, you!" Serenity threw her hands up and wrapped them around his neck.

"Hey back!" He hugged her with his one free hand, and their lips connected as routinely as if he walked into her place daily. The thought of coming home to her every day flashed across his mind. He immediately shook his head. What was wrong with him?

"Come on in the kitchen." She took his hand and bounced down the hall with him in tow.

"Serenity." He tried his best to contain his sigh. He placed the shopping bag on the counter.

"Let's hurry and get this dessert done, so I can give you my surprise." She didn't seem to notice his serious tone when he said her name. "Now show me how to make this pie that you claim to be just as good as my nana's."

"Okay, but—"

"But nothing!" she interrupted. "I won't be convinced until I taste it. Come on. These are for you." She pointed to pie pans she'd laid out on the kitchen table. "Do you need anything else?"

"No. This is fine."

Serenity clapped her hands. "Chop, chop, buddy!" She tossed her head back when she laughed.

Serenity's playful nature made the atmosphere gleeful. Chris decided not to spoil the moment. He'd tell her during dinner.

"All right." Chris shook his head and went to the sink to wash his hands. "Put the oven at 350 degrees and pay attention," he said, wiping his hands dry with a paper towel. Chris extracted from the bags the items he'd brought with him.

"Woo!" Serenity thrust both hands in the air. "Pecan pie."

She picked up her phone, and a moment later music flowed from a Bluetooth speaker. She danced over to a hook beside the stove and two-stepped back toward him with an apron. He bent his tall frame so she could fit it over his head.

He laid the ingredients across the counter and popped a pecan in his mouth.

She swatted him. "Hey! No stealing pecans—" she took a few herself and ate them "—without me."

Chris shook his head and smiled. "Are you ready to learn?"

"Yes!" Serenity sidled up close to him.

Carefully, he went through the recipe, step by step. They danced to the music barreling through the speakers as they prepared the pie. "How you make this is just as important as what you put in it. This can't be rushed, okay?"

"Okay." She watched closely.

The song changed and they swayed to that one together, finishing up the pie and pouring the filling into the pastry-lined pans. "Taste." He put a small bit on his finger and held it to her mouth.

She licked his finger, closed her eyes and moaned. "That is so good."

As they placed the pies in the heated oven, the song switched again and Serenity screamed.

"Oh! This is my favorite song." She took the spoon Chris had used to mix the ingredients and began singing into the "microphone." He laughed, loving her playful nature, but quickly realized her velvety-smooth voice was actually beautiful. He folded his arms across his chest, leaned against the counter and enjoyed her impromptu performance. She hit a high note, sounding better than the recording artist. His head reared back and his mouth fell open. Mesmerized, he stayed that way, listening until her strong finish. After the last note, she bowed. He wanted her more in that moment than he had before.

"Wow!" He shook his head slowly. Her voice reminded him of his sister Chloe's. "I…I didn't know you could sing like that." An audience of one, he applauded as he drew closer.

With Serenity at arm's length, he reached for her, searching her eyes. A force he couldn't resist compelled him to her lips. He kissed her breath away. When they parted, she pulled him to her again, wrapping her arms around his neck. Chris lifted her up. Her legs folded around his back. He held her tighter. Kissed her deeper. Yearned for her more.

The kiss grew urgent. Her hands roamed his chest,

squeezing, caressing. Chris whisked her to the counter and sat her there. Their lips remained locked. Hungry groans filled the air. Finally, they released each other's mouths, gasping for air. He swooped down on her beautiful neck, planting a trail of moist kisses there, before moving back to her lips. She groped handfuls of his shirt.

His hands found their way to her breasts. Gently, he massaged her ample mounds. Another moan rose in her throat. His body responded with a swift jerk in his groin. The temperature around them rose sharply. Time disappeared. They grasped at each other as if one of them were in danger of slipping away. She unbuttoned his shirt. They stopped kissing again, but just long enough to catch their breath.

Chris looked up at the ceiling. He had to stop now before things went too far. It was hard for him to contain his desire for her. He'd never been so close to the edge of his own resolve. Feeling his heart thump against his chest, he inhaled deeply to steady his erratic breathing. Serenity had taken to his chest, randomly planting delicious kisses—each one sending flashes of electric currents through his torso.

"Serenity." It came out as a breathless whisper. She didn't respond. "Serenity," he said again, but it was only a bit louder. He panted another moment. "Serenity."

She'd heard him this time. Her head snapped up. With a sated smile and half-cocked lids, she looked intoxicated. He knew she was just as drunk with need as he was. Immediately, he felt pressure in his groin. He wanted her bad.

"We should stop," he said between breaths. "I could go." He didn't want to rush her.

"Don't go," she pleaded but took her hands off him. Erratic breaths floated her chest up and down.

They stared into each other's eyes for a moment. Serenity turned away and smiled, seeming bashful. She wiped moisture from her upper lip. An awkward silence hung between them.

"Are you okay?" He wanted her to be.

"I'm fine." She pushed back a sprig of hair that had fallen over her eye. "What about you?"

Chris grinned and shook his head. "Never been better. We need to check the pie."

"Yes." This time her smile expressed a level of comfort. "We should."

Serenity scampered to her feet. Chris helped her. She walked the few feet to the stove, pulled the door down and looked in. He peered over her shoulder.

"It's fine," he assured her. "I'm going to run to the bathroom."

Chris looked at his reflection in the vanity mirror. His body was finally calming down. He thought about the best way to tell Serenity about his identity. There was no need to maintain discretion any longer. There was still part of him that was concerned about how she would respond, but he believed that once he explained why he'd done it that way, she'd understand. He had to tell her now, before things landed on a new level.

He came out of the bathroom and went straight to the oven and checked the pie. "Just a few more minutes." His phone rang. It was Kent. He hit Decline.

"Great," she said. "Now for your surprise."

He furrowed his brow. She took his hand and led him to her den. Dim lighting cast a mellow glow through the quaint room. In the center, a small table was set for two with flowers, candles and covered dishes. She directed him to one of the chairs and disappeared for a moment. He heard the music from the kitchen turn off, and she returned with a saxophone. She tapped icons on her cell phone and transferred the sound to the Bluetooth speaker she had in the den. His phone rang again. It was Kent once more. Silencing the phone, he turned his attention back to her.

"I don't have friends like you who can get me front-row tickets to shows at the last minute or prepare dinners in amazing settings during off-hours, but I'm capable of cooking up a mean meal and providing pretty decent dinner music." She curtsied and began to play a soft melody.

He placed his elbow on the arm of the chair and rested his chin on his fist. Was he blushing? He wasn't sure because no one had ever made him blush before. He was certain about feeling grateful and quite lucky. He allowed himself to be taken up by the rhythm. Not only could she sing well, but she was also a great sax player.

Chris watched the way Serenity licked the reed, moistening it with her tongue. That simple, common gesture now set something in his core ablaze. Focusing on her mouth, he surveyed her closely, paying special attention to the way her lips wrapped around the instrument. Warmth passed through him and settled between his legs. His manhood awakened and a flash of urgency shot through him.

He stood and slowly carried himself toward her as if he were driven by a force he was unable to resist. At first he swayed with her as she played a sweet jazzy riff. They held one another in a gaze that sizzled with sensual electricity. For several moments they floated together with the melody she created.

Serenity stopped playing. Their eyes locked. Before she could bring the sax back to her mouth, Chris swooped in and covered her lips with his, kissing her breath away again. He couldn't help himself. His need of her was so strong in that moment. He took the sax, placed it on the nearby chair and wrapped his arms around her. She followed suit and embraced him back.

The fire they created crackled, passing from one to the other as their mouths connected. She held him tighter. He pressed his rising erection against her belly. Serenity pressed against him, ridding all space between their bodies. The atmosphere grew even warmer. Serenity's caresses became hungry grasps. She groped for his neck and chest, and roamed his taut back and backside as far as she could reach.

They pried themselves apart to breathe. She closed her eyes, let her head fall back and moaned. His fiery tongue flickered against her exposed neck. She was a delicious combination of heat and sweetness. He wanted more. Immediately.

Chris lifted Serenity in his strong arms. In the next beat, her legs were wrapped around his waist. He carried her to the chaise and laid her down without disconnecting from their steamy kiss. He pulled back and looked into her eyes, seeking permission to proceed. Approval came in another greedy kiss. Serenity reached down and tugged at his belt. He helped her, releasing the restraint in one skillful yank.

Desire made his motions urgent. He moved as if they he needed to outrun time. She unbuttoned his shirt. He pulled hers over her head. She unzipped his pants. He unhooked her bra. Perfect mounds bounced free. He took them by the handful. Taking turns, he toyed with each nipple between his teeth. She groaned. He sucked harder.

Chris kissed her lips, traveled along her neck and recaptured her mounds. Next he moved to her navel and explored her body like a treasure map.

"Can I taste you?" His inquiry held more breath than voice. He needed her approval.

"Please." Yearning stretched her response into a breathy whisper.

Chris smiled, delighted that he'd been given a pass. He wanted to satisfy her well and quench his insatiable desire. More than anything, he wanted to take good care of her, have her sing his name in that beautiful voice of hers. He had never felt more compelled to please a woman. If he didn't hurry, he thought he might explode.

Chris continued his kisses past her navel, slid her lace panties down her smooth legs and dipped his tongue into the smoldering folds between her thighs. Serenity's breath caught. At the same time, her back arched with a paralyzing rigidity. She hissed a second later, and her body relaxed. He lapped at her bud with an increasing tempo until his rhythm became feverish. She squealed as juices gushed like the falls.

While Serenity's climax rippled through her, clenching her muscles in spasms, Chris quickly retrieved a condom from the wallet in his fallen jeans. Sheathing himself with a skillful quickness, he carefully entered her still-quivering body. She gripped him with her walls. The intense pleasure temporarily rendered him motionless.

Her release, still tumbling through, caused her to suction him over and over again. Chris closed his eyes and held on to keep from being overtaken by the pleasure that threatened to coax an early climax to the surface. Slowly at first, he moved through the cushioning until she could relax. They fell in sync. He picked up the pace, gradually increasing his tempo. Together they reached new levels of intensity, calling each other's names, bucking against one another. She cried out first. He grunted with each buck, creating a staccato song until one long war cry escaped. He collapsed on top of her. Both bodies fell limp.

Chris held her tight. Serenity held him back. And they were done. It was as delectable and intense as it was quick. But they couldn't take it back now. Nor did he want to.

"Are you okay?"

"Yes." She sighed, closed her eyes and smiled. "I'm fine."

He kept watching her, hoping not to see any signs of regret. There didn't seem to be any. Her well-being in this was important.

"I knew what I was getting myself into, and I wanted it."

He felt relieved but then thought about what he had to tell her. Taking a deep breath, he held her against him, skin to skin, her breast against his chest. She nestled against him, and he pondered how to say what he had to say. He'd tell her as soon as they got dressed. Right now, he wanted to stay there with her in his arms.

Chris's phone rang. Kent was calling again. He sent the call to voice mail, and it rang again immediately after.

"Maybe you should answer that."

"It's just my friend. I can speak to him later."

"If you insist." Serenity swiped at her own phone and the music changed. "Okay, Mr. Mullins."

Her words, that name, came down on him like bricks. Chris huffed. He had to tell her now. His phone rang again.

"You really should answer that." She seemed genuinely concerned. "Something could be wrong."

"I'm sorry." He answered the call. He'd get Kent off the phone fast and focus on telling Serenity what he'd been keeping from her.

"Chris, we have a problem." Kent's troubled tone made him stand straight.

"What's wrong?" Concern filled her expression. She gently placed her hand on his arm.

"There's been a fire at the bar. The fire department is here now. It's bad."

"I'm on my way." Chris huffed. "I'm sorry, Serenity. There's an emergency." He snatched his shirt off the floor and shot his hands through the arms.

"Is there anything I can do?" Serenity walked behind him, trying to keep pace.

"No, but thanks!" He stuffed his legs into his pants one by one and then kissed her lips. For a quick moment, he stared into her worried eyes.

"Do you need me to come with you?"

Chris smiled. "I'll be fine." He headed for the door, stopped and turned back for one more kiss. Serenity melted in his arms.

"Call me, okay? If not I'll worry."

"I will. I'm sorry. I'll make it up to you, okay?"

"No need."

"When I get back, there's something that I want talk to you about."

"What is it?" Serenity looked puzzled.

A peck on her lips was his only answer. Chris wasn't prepared to say much more without getting too far into it. "I'll be back tonight."

# Chapter 15

The week ended, but that didn't mean that work was done for Serenity. She and Elisa handled bridal shower plans and picked out favors. Serenity submitted the grant application for Heartstrings, led music lessons and squeezed in a conference call with the board to go over updates on the gala.

Between her schedule and Chris having to deal with the fire, they hadn't laid eyes on each other all week. The late-night chats were diminished by fatigue from long, full days. Several times Serenity came home, fell into bed and didn't wake until her alarm clock invaded her sleep the next morning. Saturday proved to be just as busy as the weekdays had been for both of them. Chris insisted on coming over to spend the entire day with her on Sunday. She couldn't wait to enjoy his company. It didn't take long for his absence to feel like a void. Each time he told her they needed to "talk," she wondered why he refused to give any hints about what was on his mind. He told her that their discussion had to happen face-to-face. She had no idea what it was about but was intrigued nonetheless.

She blushed as she turned in the mirror to check her

gown. A smile instinctively framed her mouth when she thought about Chris. She wished he could join her at the gala she was preparing to attend, but he'd already told her he had an engagement, so she hadn't bothered to ask. Besides, she'd received her invite the day before, when a friend's boyfriend had to back out due to a last-minute work trip. That friend had encouraged her to accompany her to the gala because of the impressive guest list—several key contacts who could all be instrumental in helping Heartstrings grow.

Serenity dug in her closet and slipped on a pair of blue sandals that were the same hue as her dress. They would raise her to an average height. She took one last look in the mirror. Her upswept hair was easy but elegant. Teardrop pearls hung gracefully from her ears, and a single strand of pearls lay tastefully across her neck. She grabbed a shawl to protect her bare shoulders against the chill in the evening air, picked up her ivory satin purse and headed for the car.

Serenity turned the ignition, then heard buzzing and dug for her vibrating phone. She pulled it from the purse and answered through the car's Bluetooth system.

"Hey, you." An instinctive smile spread across her lips.

"All is well now that I'm hearing your voice."

The blushing began. "How sweet!"

"I just have a moment, but I wanted to talk to you about tomorrow. Don't prepare anything. It will be my turn to prepare a meal for you."

"If you insist."

"Okay. I got to run. See you tomorrow, pretty lady."

Serenity's cheeks burned red. "See you tomorrow, Mr. Mullins."

Ending the call, Serenity checked her mirror and

pulled out of her parking spot. The catering hall was only fifteen minutes away. Setting her satellite radio to her favorite jazz station, she bobbed her head to the rhythm as she drove, instinctively identifying notes and instruments in her head.

Minutes later, she pulled into the circular drive of the establishment, stepped out and gave the valet her keys. When she walked inside, a tall gentleman with wispy blond hair raised a brow with an approving smile. She smiled back and headed to the bar for a glass of wine, then searched for her colleague.

"Serenity!"

She turned, trying to gauge the direction of the voice.

"Over here."

A fellow teacher and savvy socialite waved. Serenity lifted her glass, acknowledging her, and headed that way.

"Stephanie." Serenity leaned forward and gave her a friendly kiss on the cheek.

"You look absolutely stunning!" Stephanie stood back and twirled her finger. "Turn around."

Serenity twirled.

Stephanie shook her head in disbelief. "You're truly my inspiration. How much weight did you lose?"

"Forty pounds."

"I wish I had the discipline."

"The weight is one thing. That whole moderation issue…" Serenity rolled her eyes. "That's my daily struggle. I'm a real foodie, and sometimes the things that taste best are the worst. Getting your mind to accept the new you is another situation. I still pick up clothes in my old size, if I'm not paying attention."

"Pfft! I wish I had that problem." Stephanie twisted her lips. "Come." She grabbed Serenity's hand. "Let me introduce you to a few people."

Serenity followed her to a beautiful woman with warm, brown eyes, who was in a striking silver gown.

"Jade! I'd like you to meet my friend Serenity. She runs an amazing nonprofit organization called Heartstrings. They do incredible work for underserved youth in the areas of music and the arts." Stephanie turned to Serenity. "Jade Chandler is the executive director of the Chandler Foundation."

"It's a pleasure to meet you, Serenity. I love your name."

"And I love your dress. It's a pleasure to meet you as well, Jade."

Someone called Jade's name. The way she whipped her head toward the beckon reminded Serenity of a shampoo commercial.

Jade nodded and turned back toward Serenity and Stephanie. "I'm sorry. I'm being summoned." She pulled a card from her purse and handed it to Serenity. "I'd love to hear more about your organization."

"I'd be happy to tell you more." Serenity handed Jade a card, as well.

"Great!" Her smile was sweet. "And, Stephanie, I'll see you this weekend, right?"

"Wouldn't miss it for the world."

Jade trotted off. Stephanie leaned toward Serenity's ear. "She's loaded. The foundation is the nonprofit arm of Chandler Food Corp."

"She's a Chandler? As in Chandler Food Corp? As in Mary Kate's pies?" Serenity's eyes widened. "Their pecan pies are the best."

"Yep."

"I submitted a grant proposal to them this past week. I sure hope I get it."

"Well, you better use the contact information on that

card soon. You know this world is all about who you know, and the rich give money to people they like."

A spark of excitement shot up Serenity's spine. If she didn't meet anyone else tonight, she'd go home happy. Carefully, she tucked Jade's card into her purse and made a mental note to reach out to her and suggest they meet for lunch. She'd love an opportunity to give her more insight about the organization.

Stephanie waved at someone across the room. "Come on. Let's go meet Henry. That old guy has so much money, he can wipe with it and never miss a dollar. His family is in the banking industry, and they run the Hagerman Foundation."

"How do you know all of these people?" Serenity whispered.

"Honey, Long Island is a small place. The wealthy operate within intimate circles and do all the same things. No one wants to be outshone."

"You grew up in this world. What made you become a teacher and not go into your family's manufacturing business?"

"I love kids and simpler living." Stephanie's smile widened as she approached Henry.

His white hair and beard gave him a warm presence, despite his looming height.

"Stephanie." Henry opened his long arms, inviting her into his embrace. "How's your dad? I haven't seen him on the green lately. What is he—scared?" His laughter boomed.

"That sounds like a challenge, Mr. Hagerman!"

"Indeed it is." He lifted his chin. "And who is this pretty lady?"

"My good friend and fellow teacher, Serenity Wil-

liams." They shook as Stephanie boasted about Heartstrings once again.

"Hmm." Henry seemed sincerely interested. Sticking
his hand in his pocket, he pulled out a card. "Give me a
call Monday morning. Let's talk about how we might be
able to work together. If you're a friend of Stephanie…"
Henry finished his statement with an adoring look at
Stephanie. She tilted her head and smiled. "I've known
this young lady since she was a toddler."

"That's wonderful. And thank you. I will certainly
give you a call." Serenity held up his card before slipping it into her purse.

"Enjoy the gala, Mr. Hagerman. We have a few more
rounds to make before they begin ushering us into the
banquet hall."

"Surely. See you around, my dear." He turned to Serenity. "It was a pleasure meeting you."

Serenity acknowledged his kind smile with a nod. "It
was a pleasure meeting you too, sir."

"Please. Call me Henry."

"I sure will."

Serenity waited until they were out of earshot. "My
goodness, Stephanie. Both of those were great contacts.
Thanks so much. I'm already glad that I came."

"See? I told you."

The soothing sound of chimes floated throughout the
room. A tall gentleman dressed in a black tux ushered
them to a large ballroom in a commanding but pleasant
voice, fit for announcements.

Guests poured through the doors from the cocktail
reception to the dining area, where the main event was
being held. Stephanie led Serenity to a reserved table
right near the podium and excused herself. Serenity

watched the people milling about in search of their seats and noticed that Jade sat at the table next to them.

Looking around the room made Serenity feel hopeful. One day her small organization would be large enough to hold an event like this one. Her gala would grow up to be as grand as this. She imagined the podium sign depicting Heartstrings' logo, the shimmer of brilliant chandeliers sparkling overhead, ornate fixings all around the room that would be packed with guests ready to donate large amounts for the work her organization was doing.

"One day," she said under her breath.

First she needed to get this current program funded. It would be the largest one her company ever received. Serenity had already spoken to her principal about the possible leave of absence, but that was before they had laid off the other music teacher and filled Serenity's schedule with extra classes. They would certainly have to find someone else to fill that void. She'd have to leave for Brazil in July and wouldn't return until December, when school ended for their summer break.

Retreating into her thoughts, she'd zoned out the people around her. When she looked up, the room was filled with the scurry of men handsomely dressed in fine tuxes and women in elegant gowns. A gentleman far across the room reminded her of Chris. Waving off the possibility, she returned to her thoughts, but the man she'd just seen brought Chris to the forefront of her mind. If the grant request were to be funded, she'd have to say goodbye to him. She shook her head. Becoming comfortable with Chris had happened so fast. She'd love to explore the depths of where they could go as a couple, but how would she handle being away from him for so long? The distance would be agonizing. She missed him this past week, and he was in the same county. At least she thought he was. Serenity tilted her head and frowned. It dawned on her that she didn't know where he lived.

Serenity knew so much about him from their extensive conversations—his family, goals, dreams, likes, dislikes, etc. Yet there were still some things she didn't know. She'd meant to ask more about why he wasn't on social media. Google hadn't produced anything conclusive or alarming, and she was thankful that no mug shots appeared. The name seemed common enough. She could tell from his profile on the dating site that he preferred to stay low-key. She understood that perfectly. Maybe she'd convince him to start a Facebook account. That is, of course, if he wasn't like her cousin who refused to engage in any social media platforms.

"Whew!" Stephanie returned to the table like a brush of wind. "I had to run back to my car to get my shawl. As comfortable as this room is, I knew I'd get cold." She sat gracefully and took a deep breath. "Running in heels is never recommended. How are you doing?"

"I'm great. Just taking in the scenery. I'd love to have my gala here one day."

"You should."

"Good evening, ladies and gentleman..." A voice broke into their conversation, capturing the attention of both Serenity and Stephanie. "And welcome to the fifteenth annual Crescent Ball. On behalf of the Hagerman Foundation, I'd like to thank each of you for joining us tonight."

Applause erupted in the audience. The woman introduced herself as the executive director, and Serenity listened keenly to every word she said. She'd structure her speech the same way, she determined. Dinner was served and the program continued. Serenity noted a few ideas for her upcoming gala. The scale wasn't the same, but she could make some things work on a smaller level.

The woman called the audience's attention to the screens mounted to the walls around the room. A musical crescendo rose, followed by a booming voice touting highlights and accomplishments of the night's honorees. The first was a family-court judge, who spent her spare time serving youth throughout surrounding communities. The second was a medical professional, who had started a free clinic in a low-income neighborhood. Serenity was impressed with the exhaustive list of accomplishments of these fairly young professionals. It was the last honoree that rendered her speechless.

When his face appeared on the screen next to a name she didn't recognize, she was temporarily frozen in her own confusion—doubting what she saw. Serenity shook her head as if doing so would reset reality. She peered at the screen. The face was Chris's but the last name was different. She looked around the room in search of Chris. There had to be an error. The resemblance was uncanny. She waited for the video to finish. Chris stood up from the table on the other side of the podium and strutted toward the other honorees standing near the emcee. Jade Chandler whooped and applauded with several others at the same table, who were all standing on their feet cheering Chris on.

It was him. All doubts had been erased. Serenity was clear about what she saw. His debonair gait was unmistakable. The man she'd grown to adore and spent so much time with wasn't who he'd presented himself to be. Christopher Mullins was really Christian Chandler of *the* Chandler Food Corp. Another woman would have been ecstatic, finding that they'd come upon a prince, but Serenity was furious.

She stood abruptly, knocking the table with her thigh. Water glasses teetered and threatened to spill over the side, dishes clinked. Her tablemates looked at her with inquiries in their eyes. She ignored them. With a heaving chest, she narrowed her gaze toward the three standing honorees. It was Chris for sure. An angry heat spread over her ears and cheeks.

"Serenity," Stephanie whispered, touching her arm gently.

Serenity heard her but didn't answer. She kept her eyes trained on Chris. He stepped up to accept his beautiful crescent-shaped award and approached the podium. With a charming smile, he scanned the audience. Their eyes met and the smile slid down his face. His mouth hung open. Serenity glared, recognizing his shock. He recovered quickly and with a nervous chuckle started his acceptance speech.

She grabbed her purse, excused herself and marched toward the exit. She'd explain things to Stephanie later. Right now she needed air.

Barging through the bathroom door, Serenity went straight to the last stall. Locking the door, she paced the small space, questioning her own judgment. What was she missing? Why did she keep attracting liars in her life?

Though she hadn't used the bathroom, she washed her hands and left. She handed the young, freckle-faced valet her ticket. As he ran off, she took a deep breath and then looked down. A heated surge of energy pulsated through her restless limbs. She tapped her foot as she waited for the valet, wanting him to hurry so she could get away from that banquet hall.

Finally, the young man pulled up, stepped out and handed Serenity her keys. She reached into her purse for a tip and pressed it into his hand, before climbing into her car.

"Serenity, wait!"

With one leg in, she paused. Looking over the roof of her car, she spotted Chris coming her way. Cutting her eyes at him, she got inside and fumbled with the mirrors. She wanted to pull off before he made it over to her but couldn't get her fingers to cooperate effectively. She looked into the mirrors as she positioned them. He was getting closer. She pulled the seat belt across her body and jammed it into the slot. He knocked on the driver's-side window. Serenity groped at the gears, finally getting it right. She slammed the car into Drive and pulled off hard. The car lurched, and the tires screeched.

From the rearview mirror, she could see him standing with his hands up. She turned onto the main street. The maneuver was anything but smooth.

"Why did he have to be a liar too?"

## Chapter 16

"What was that about?" Jade asked, when Chris returned to the banquet hall.

"That was just an old friend." Chris's hands were perched on his hips. He still hadn't caught his breath and paced small circles around himself.

"You don't look like you just had a friendly exchange."

"Not now, Jade. Please." Chris huffed. His heart was still pounding. "I'll be right back."

He wasn't sure where he was going but needed to go somewhere before the rest of his family started asking more questions. The entire Chandler crew had come out to see him receive his award. Chris found his way to the gazebo several feet from the back entrance. Sitting on the stone bench, he placed his head in his hands.

The last person he had expected to see was Serenity. He had planned to explain everything to her the next day while preparing a nice dinner but doubted she'd be interested in seeing him now. Walking away would be easy. He could just let this incident fade away, but denying the truth didn't make sense. It didn't take long to see that she was one of the great ones. She possessed everything he liked in a woman, as well as a few things he hadn't realized he appreciated until they'd met.

Even if this was the end for them, he felt a need to explain himself. Chris had been known for lots of things, but a liar was never one of them. He'd understand if she never wanted to see him again, but he needed to explain.

He stood, tugged his suit jacket and marched through the banquet hall and straight out the front door. A young attendant jogged up to him, and Chris handed over his ticket. Moments later, he maneuvered his sports car through the streets at top speed, cutting the fifteen-minute ride to Serenity's house down to ten minutes.

The car jerked to a stop. He had barely put the car in Park before snatching the keys out. Hastening his steps, he reached her door quickly but stood a moment before knocking. He hadn't prepared his words. For the first time, he felt as though he didn't know what to say. Another deep breath, and he gently knocked on her door. Serenity didn't respond. He knocked harder and at the same time rang the bell. Allowing a few more moments to pass, he banged with the side of his fist. An older woman walking a small dog stopped and glared at him. He smiled and waved. She scrutinized him with one squinted eye for a moment and then continued walking.

He banged again. "Please. Serenity. I can explain." Somehow he knew she could hear him. "Open the door." Chris looked back at her spot. Her car was there. "I'm not leaving until I get a chance to talk to you. I'm not a liar."

"Yes, you are!" Serenity shouted through the door.

"I thought you weren't home."

"This isn't funny, Chris."

"Please…" Chris took another deep breath. "Just open the door. I'll tell you why I did this, and then you can kick me out and never see me again, if that's what you want."

Several moments passed, and then Chris heard the click of the locks. The door groaned as she pulled it open—wide enough for a small foot to fit.

Chris sighed. "Can I come in? I won't take long."

Serenity opened the door the rest of the way and stepped aside. The dejected look on her face pained him. He hated being the cause of her unpleasant mood. She'd taken off her gown, but her curves looked just as sexy in leggings and a tank top.

Gingerly, Chris stepped in. He leaned forward to give Serenity a customary kiss on the cheek. She looked away and folded her arms across her chest. Pressing his lips together, he raised his brows. Could he blame her?

"Can we sit and talk?"

Without a word, she dropped her arms and walked into the living room. He followed closely behind. She sat hard, leaned back and refolded her arms. He took his seat on the love seat at the opposite side of the room.

After a deep breath, he pulled his wallet from his pocket, opened it and placed his license on the ottoman. "My name is Christian Chandler. People close to me call me Chris. My family owns Chandler Food Corp." He watched for her reaction. "I never meant to deceive you." He paused again. Her expression remained stoic. "The reason I used a fake name is because I wanted to find out what it would be like to date a woman who wasn't enamored with the fact that I was a Chandler."

Serenity raised a brow.

"I kept running into women who were more concerned with the fact that I was an heir than they were about who I was as a person. I got tired of talking about my pedigree. I wondered if women would act the same if they didn't know who my family was. I wasn't a fan of on-line dating, but I tried it assuming it would be one way to meet people outside of my normal circles. I needed to know that there were still other kinds of women in this world—ones who were genuine and cared about things other than labels and how good we would look on paper as a couple."

He stopped talking. He wanted to give Serenity the space to respond. She didn't.

"But then I met you."

Her expression softened a tiny bit, but she still hadn't spoken.

"I honestly didn't expect to find you or anyone like you—fun, compassionate, beautiful, carefree. We have so much in common. You seem to get what life is really about, and you look damn good doing it. You possess the substance that I've been looking for in a woman for years. I was almost convinced that it no longer existed. I planned to tell you last week when you made dinner for me, but then the fire happened. This wasn't a conversation for the phone. That's why I wanted to come over for dinner tomorrow so I could tell you then, but then tonight happened."

Serenity unfolded her arms. Chris hoped he was getting through to her.

"Everything about you was unexpected. I'm sorry you found out like this, but I need you to know I'm not a liar." Serenity turned away. "I'm not a deceitful person. People could tell you a lot about Christian Chandler, but none would ever say I wasn't a man of integrity." After a few moments of silence, he stood and picked up his license. He released another heavy sigh. "I never meant to hurt you. If you're interested, I'd love to continue seeing you…get to know you all over again…have you meet my family…my friends. They'll confirm who I really am. But if not, I understand."

Serenity remained silent and still didn't move. Chris started toward the door.

"I'll give you some time to think about all of this."

Finally, she stood and followed him to the door. She pulled it open. He pushed it closed, startling her. Serenity's head snapped back.

"I still want to see you," he repeated. He tucked his bottom lip. But…" He swallowed the rest of his statement, feeling as though it wouldn't matter. "Good night, Serenity."

"Good night, Chris." Her tone was dry.

At least she had spoken to him, Chris thought. He left, casually making his way to the car. He had done what he had had to do—cleared the air. He reached his car, bogged down by thoughts of what he'd supposedly lost in this situation. Once inside, he started the ignition but sat for a while before pulling off. It surprised him how Serenity had come into his life and intrigued him so much in a matter of weeks. He hadn't driven for more than a few minutes before he felt a void.

# Chapter 17

Serenity watched through the window as he left. Once he walked beyond her view, she went to her room and crawled in bed, folding into a ball. This was exactly why she didn't want to do that silly online dating. She thought about calling Elisa and letting her have it, but she was too torn to rein in her emotions. Chris had left her feeling confused. Being upset about his lie was justifiable. However, his story seemed legit, and he appeared to be sincere. She didn't know what to believe. Serenity grabbed her phone and dialed Rayne's number.

"Hey, lady! You're home already? How was the ball?"

"A disaster. Hold on, let me get Elisa on the phone." Serenity hit Add Call, rolled through her contacts, and selected Elisa's name. Seconds later she was on the line.

"What's up?"

"Hold on for Rayne and me." Serenity merged the calls.

"Now, what's going on? What made the ball a disaster?" Rayne asked.

"Did something happen?" Elisa asked.

Serenity started with the awards and explained every-thing that had transpired.

"Whoa!" Elisa said. "What did you say?"

"Basically nothing. I didn't know what to say."

"I can imagine," Rayne said. "What are you going to do?"

"What is there to do? It's over."

"It doesn't have to be."

"What? Elisa, you know how I feel about men who are liars."

"It really doesn't sound like he intended to deceive you. I can see why he did this. He came clean."

"That's after I found out. Who knows what other lies he's told? I can't trust him."

"I don't know," Rayne said. "This is hard. I under-stand you being upset, but I also understand where he's coming from."

"He's a Chandler, for goodness' sake. And he's quite handsome. I can only imagine the scores of woman scheming to get him to put a ring on it."

"This isn't funny, Elisa."

"I wasn't trying to be funny. Think about it. This man can have any woman and, from the sound of it, he wants you."

"I don't care if he's rich. I want someone I can trust."

"Did he seem sincere when he explained why he used the fake name?" Rayne asked.

"Yeah, but so what?"

"Then maybe—just maybe—he actually was."

"Consider this," Elisa interjected. "If it ended now, would you have any regrets?" Serenity thought about Elisa's question. "Would you be willing to give him a chance to prove himself?"

Serenity groaned. "I don't know. He said he wanted

to continue seeing me but would understand if I didn't want to take this any further."

"I say you continue dating him and see what happens," Elisa said. "Think about it. He's got a lot to prove to you. He knows he could never get caught in another lie because then he'd never regain your trust. What would you have to lose?"

"I don't know about this."

"I agree with Rayne. If he seemed sincere, give him a chance. His argument is actually legit. It's just like us. We got tired of dealing with men who seemed to be only interested in sex. If there was something we could do to detect their true intentions, we'd do it, right?"

"I guess." Serenity rolled onto her back and placed her free hand on her forehead.

"Sleep on it," Rayne suggested.

"I will."

Elisa giggled. "This is so *Coming to America.* Instead of getting a prince, you're getting an heir. If you two get married, I want a boatload of those Mary Kate's pies they sell in the supermarket. You should have dancers at your wedding like they did in the movie."

"Elisa!" Serenity chided. Rayne's distinct cackle barreled through the phone. Elisa joined her. Serenity tried to stay composed but failed and laughed along with them.

"You're nuts, Elisa. I don't care about his money."

"I know, but it's a pretty damn good perk!"

"Good night, ladies. Thanks for always being there."

Serenity ended the call, rolled over and put her cell phone on the nightstand. She wasn't any closer to deciding what to do. The points that Rayne and Elisa had brought up were the same ones she'd volleyed in her head. Still, she didn't want to be made a fool of. She grabbed her pillow in a viselike grip and grunted. Maybe she'd sleep on it and figure out what to do in the morning.

She got up and walked through the house, turning off lights and checking locks. Back in her room, she slid her leggings off and climbed into bed. An hour later, sleep still evaded her. Her mind grappled with how to handle the situation. Valid reasons for both sides fought for precedence. Memories of their late-night talks, their amazing first date and the Sunday before also kept her from slumber. Not a day had gone by without her hearing from Chris since their initial connection. He had taken the time to teach her how to make pecan pie, and it was delicious. That was special. No man had ever done something like that with her. Chris encouraged her passions, telling her how she could indulge them. Her ex hadn't done that. When he looked at pictures of her before the weight loss, he told her she was beautiful then and hadn't flinched.

Serenity remembered how they had made love Sunday, how her body craved him and how he satisfied every whim. Her core involuntarily shuddered. His kisses had made her feel as though she was standing on clouds. These thoughts weren't helping. She didn't want to miss him. Clear thinking was what she needed to focus on right now.

The hour grew later until the new day arrived. Moonlight from the midnight sky glowed through her window shades. As tired as she was, she couldn't turn her mind off. If she could just rest, maybe her mind would be clear enough to make a decision.

Serenity patted the nightstand for her phone, opened a music app and set it on soft jazz. Focusing on the notes, she calmed her mind enough to finally fall asleep, but she still couldn't get away from Chris. He showed up in her dreams.

## Chapter 18

Chris awoke tired. Fitful sleep had kept him from getting any rest, and his sisters hadn't helped any. All three showed up last night, arriving at his house moments after he got back from Serenity's, and demanded explanations. Jewel brought his award to him. He hadn't realized he'd left it until she set it on his console table.

Like sisters, they made themselves as comfortable as possible in their evening gowns, pulling popcorn and chips from his cabinets and copping squats in his den. Knowing he didn't have much of a choice, he filled them in on what had happened. He would have called Kent and Ray but knew they were managing a crowd at The Reserve, after getting the kitchen to a point where they could prepare meals, after the fire. There were still renovations needed, but at least they were able to open back up by the end of the week with some new equipment in place. The fire hadn't done enough damage to put them out of business completely, but managing the cleanup had taken all their extra time that week.

"You've got some proving to do if you want to win her back," Jewel had told him last night.

"If you really care about her, don't give up so easily. Give her a moment to absorb all of this, but let her know you want her and will make it up to her." Chloe always gave advice with substance. She was such a big sister.

"Let me talk to her," Jade offered.

All three of them held their hands up and said, "No!" at the same time.

"I'll handle it," Chris promised.

"Be sure to make her feel special if she gives you a second chance," Jade added.

After that they hung out for a while longer before Chris retreated to bed. Serenity forgave him in his dreams. When he woke, he knew that he could possibly face a different reality.

Pushing back the covers, Chris got up, brushed his teeth and changed into sweatpants and a tank top. He went to his garage, set music to flow from the hidden speakers and worked out in the area he had redesigned as a gym. Pumping weights and a quick run on the treadmill helped to relieve some stress and get his day started. After a long, hot shower, he slipped on a fresh pair of sweats and checked his phone. There was a text message from Serenity.

I'm trying to see this from your side.

For Chris, that was an in. It was time to put his sisters' advice to work. He texted her back.

Maybe I can help. Can I come over?

Chris waited but there was no immediate response. Putting the phone down, he went to the kitchen to make himself breakfast. It wasn't until after he'd eaten that she responded with Sure. Chris took a breath. He was going to win her completely over. With a fair shot, he knew things could work with them. For the first time ever, he was willing to put in the work. Moreover, he actually didn't mind.

Serenity was making him court her, progressing through each stage with patience and poise. That lost art intrigued him. They'd shared weeks of emails, before texts and phone conversations and finally meeting in person. He would have bedded his other women by now and, despite spending more time with them up front, he knew Serenity in ways that he'd never known some of the women before her.

Chris was sure about himself and knew what he wanted. He wanted Serenity. He often got what he wanted and, with a second chance, this time would be no different.

He changed his clothes, stopped by the supermarket and made his way to Serenity's house by the afternoon, giving her time to get home from church with her parents. She was still in a dress that hugged her beautiful curves when he arrived. She let him in, led him to the kitchen and excused herself, returning moments later barefoot in jeans and a graphic T-shirt.

Already familiar with her kitchen, Chris pulled the groceries from the bags and started preparing his dinner of roasted veggies, his version of Greek fingerling potatoes and wild-caught Alaskan salmon. He'd purchased one of his family's fruit pies for dessert.

Serenity put on music, washed her hands and attempted to help Chris with dinner.

"No. Thanks. Take this." He handed her a flute of sparkling wine. "Sit and allow me to do this for you."

Serenity shrugged. "Okay."

Until then, conversation between them had remained light—an awkward duet.

Once everything was on the stove and in the oven, Chris joined her at the table. "How can I help you understand?"

Serenity sighed and let her head fall back. Staring at the ceiling, she shook her head. "I'm not sure." She looked directly at him as if she were seeking sincerity in his eyes. "I'm still surprised you're here."

"You said it was okay to come."

"I know. I'm torn."

"Let me help bring it all together. I'm a man of integrity, and I'm going to prove that to you. There will never be another lie between us." Chris took her by the hand. Serenity flinched. Her discomfort bothered him. "It hasn't been long, but time isn't everything. Nor is it a qualifier for moving forward in a relationship. When things are right, they're just right, and there's something about you that feels right to me. All I want from you is to give us the chance to see this unfold. Can you do that?"

Serenity tucked her lips. Chris watched her chest move up and down. Several beats passed before she said, "Okay, but if you make a fool of me, Mr. Mul—" Chris's eyes widened "—Mr. Chandler," Serenity corrected herself, "I'll make you pay."

"I have a confession."

Serenity lifted her hands and let them fall on the table with a thump. "I don't think I can handle any more of your confessions, Chris."

His smile was a teasing one. "I cringed every time you called me 'Mr. Mullins.'"

Playfully, she rolled her eyes. "Where did you get that name from anyway?"

"It's the town my grandparents grew up in, down in South Carolina."

Serenity shook her head and tossed him a chiding glare.

"You're beautiful when you're annoyed."

She pursed her lips.

Chris got up and moved to the chair right next to Serenity. "Did you know that things are always better the second time around?"

She peered at him over the rim of her flute. Gently, he took the glass from her hand and delicately placed it on the table. She looked at him inquiringly. He held her chin in his hand, leaned forward and pressed his lips against hers. At first she remained still, and he didn't move, and she gave in, puckering against his lips. With his tongue, he parted hers and kissed her deeper. The kiss felt good to him. He didn't want to let her go. They continued until they had to break for breath.

With his forehead against hers, he said softly, "I'm sorry."

"I forgive you," she whispered.

They spent the next hour kissing and regaining their lost sense of comfort. When dinner was ready, Chris plated their meals and fed her. She smiled after every bite of dessert. His chest swelled as a result of being responsible for her smile again.

After eating, they cleared the table and cleaned the kitchen together.

"Now what?" Serenity asked, flopping on the love seat in the spare room she'd converted into a den. She pointed the remote at the television.

"Get ready to meet the Chandlers?"

Serenity's mouth fell open.

# Chapter 19

Serenity couldn't believe she was actually in the car on her way to meet Chris's parents. She'd lived on Long Island since she was a child and had never ventured to some of its northern parts. The scenery looked different from the areas on the South Shore that she frequented, changing from cozy, single-family homes and wide streets to winding roads with singular properties as large as several houses on her block combined. Grand estates hid behind ornate gates and lush greenery. Some properties were set so far from the street they required their own private roads to reach them.

Chris held her hand and spoke to her as they drove, but she was too enthralled by the massive estates, private ranches and exquisite landscaping to focus on what he was saying. Where did this man's family live? This felt like an enchanted journey.

"Here we are," Chris said, pulling into a property that rivaled the size of the middle school she'd attended.

"Whoa!" Serenity sat up, careful to take in every morsel of the magnificent view. The driveway wound around the side of the property to the front of a three-car garage.

Three other cars were parked in the same area, and there was room for at least two more. What she could see of the backyard reminded her of family trips to the Poconos. Sprawling landscapes ran into a wall of trees. They had their very own forest.

Chris parked, jumped out and opened her door. Taking her by the hand, he led her through a side entrance.

"Mom! Dad!" Chris called out, leading Serenity through the colossal home by the hand.

"In here, dear." Serenity assumed that was his mother.

Three beautiful women, who looked like female versions of Chris, came into the kitchen sporting huge smiles. She remembered Jade from the gala.

"Serenity?" The first held her hand out. "I'm Chloe, Chris's oldest sister. I hear that you have a great voice."

Serenity widened her eyes at Chris and smiled. "Yes, I hear you do, as well. It's very nice to meet you." The fact that Chris's family already knew much about her made her blush.

"Outta my way, sissy." The younger version of Chloe pushed her aside. Her cut-up jeans, tank top and ponytail positioned at the crown of her head gave her a more youthful appearance without the makeup and evening gown. "I'm Jade, remember? It's great to see you again."

"And I'm Jewel." Dressed in all black, her flirty shirt and leggings made her seem sassy and elegant at the same time. "I'm the brilliant one!"

"Puh-lease!" Jade elbowed her.

Chloe rolled her eyes and laughed. "Truthfully, she's the nutty one."

Jade nodded in agreement, shaking her head. "Yes, she is."

Jewel playfully swatted both of them.

"Step aside, so I can meet this young lady." A refined

woman, dressed in light blue slacks and a matching cashmere sweater, glided into the room. Pushing the rim of
her glasses down, she peered at Serenity over the top.

Serenity stiffened under her scrutiny. "You must be
Mrs. Chandler. It's a pleasure to meet you."

"Mmm-hmm." El Chandler examined her a little further before opening her arms and waving Serenity in.
Cautiously, Serenity moved closer, and El wrapped her
arms around her. "The pleasure is mine, darling. You
have no idea. I was wondering when my Chris would
bring another woman to meet us."

The sisters laughed, and Serenity joined them.

"Is this the lovely lady?" A voiced boomed.

"You must be Mr. Chandler." Serenity nodded respectfully at the tall, distinguished-looking gentleman.

"The last time I checked." His laughter could have
shaken the fine home to its core. "It's wonderful to meet
you, my dear." Mr. Chandler kissed the back of Serenity's hand.

"Hey, Dad. Back off," Chris teased.

"It's great to meet you as well, Mr. Chandler. You have
a beautiful home."

"Thank you." Mr. Chandler nodded. "I did all the dec-
orating myself," he said with a slick smile. Mrs. Chandler pursed her lips and narrowed her eyes to mere slits.
Mr. Chandler's sheepish laugh made all of them crack
up. He put his arm around his wife, towering over her.
"Okay. She did it all herself." He kissed the top of Mrs.
Chandler's head.

"Let's all go into the family room," El said. "Chris,
get the lovely lady something to drink."

"Stephanie introduced us at the gala last night, right?"
Jade asked.

"Yes. She's a great friend."

The warm welcome put Serenity at ease. As she walked through the house, she tried to contain her awe. By the time they'd reached the family room, she'd lost count of all the other rooms she passed by, and that was only the main floor. Her entire apartment could fit in their kitchen and dining room. She'd never seen a home that huge in real life. Yet, as big as it was, it still felt cozy.

Once they were all seated, they spent the next few hours getting to know one another. Despite the obvious difference in lifestyle, Serenity felt comfortable in their presence. Several times throughout the evening, she spotted Chris gazing at her. When she caught him, he'd smile or wink. One time, his sisters noticed the subtle exchange and looked at each other with raised brows. They asked questions about teaching and her organization, and they told her the history of the Chandler family legacy. She was impressed by his parents' humble beginnings and promised to patronize the grandparents' quaint restaurant on the South Shore.

"We never could get them to move here with us," Mrs. Chandler said, shaking her head as if the effort was exhausting.

"Maybe one day," Mr. Chandler added, patting Mrs. Chandler's hand.

The tender way he regarded his wife made Serenity smile.

Chris looked at his watch. "I need to get Serenity home." He stood and stretched. "I'll see you guys in the morning."

"Good night, dear." El wrapped her arms around Chris and then Serenity.

He gave his father a firm shake and kissed each sister.

"I need to head out too. Donovan's flight gets in around nine thirty," Chloe said.

"He's been traveling a lot lately, hasn't he?" Mrs. Chandler asked.

"Yeah. They're finalizing plans for their second hotel in Puerto Rico. You all have to come down with us for the grand opening. Serenity, have you been to Puerto Rico?"

"Not yet, but it's on my list."

"Then you should come with us. My fiancé and his partners are opening up a new resort there. It's going to be amazing."

They were all talking as if Serenity and Chris were already an official item. "That sounds wonderful." Her noncommittal reply was polite, but this was day one of meeting the family. She wouldn't allow her hopes to climb too high. Chris had some proving to do, but Serenity had to admit that he was off to a great start.

"It was great getting to know you, Serenity," Chloe said, grabbing her purse.

"Ditto!" Jade said, standing, as well. She gave Serenity a kiss on her cheek. "I'm out of here too. Gotta get up early tomorrow. Bye, Mom. Bye, Dad." Jade continued her round of kisses.

After everyone had said their goodbyes, Serenity and Chris were back in the car, heading toward her house.

"You have a really nice family."

"They're pretty cool. My sisters can be a pain in my butt sometimes, but they come in handy."

"What?" Serenity giggled. "You're so wrong for that."

Chris laced his fingers between hers. The energy between them was pleasantly familiar as if they'd been seeing each other for several years. She'd never imagined that responding to his message on a dating site would lead to this moment, this week or this day. He had actually introduced her to his parents. That was a huge step considering the small amount of time. This relationship was going somewhere fast. Besides the identity glitch, she was enjoying the pace. Chris was right—when it felt right, time didn't matter.

Cocooned in companionable silence, Serenity watched the scenery go by like a silent film. Her hand was still in Chris's. She couldn't help but feel like she'd happened upon a prince. He was handsome, charming and apparently had grown up in a darn castle, by Serenity's terms. She could get lost in his family's house for days. She glanced over at him. His eyes were glued to the dark road. Though he hadn't turned to her, he smiled and squeezed her hand, acknowledging her attention. Serenity rested her head against the chair, closed her eyes, sighed and smiled.

She awoke disoriented. She looked up and saw that Chris had parked facing the door to her apartment. "Did I fall asleep?"

"Yep. You snore like a hibernating bear!"

Serenity gasped. Her hand flew to her mouth. Her face burned with embarrassment. "Really?"

Chris laughed. "No. I was kidding."

"Chris," she whined. "Did I really?"

"No, you didn't."

Serenity swatted him. "You're so wrong for that too." She adjusted herself in the seat and squinted at her watch. "How long have we been here?"

"About ten minutes."

"Why didn't you wake me?"

"You were sleeping so well—and beautifully."

A demure smile spread across her lips. "It was nice meeting your family." There was more she wanted to say about that but held her tongue. What did this really mean for them?

"I'm glad you had a good time."

A yawn escaped her, and she quickly covered her mouth. "Oh! Excuse me. I guess I should get going. Thanks for a nice day. Dinner was great, and meeting your family was amazing. Your sisters are hilarious."

Chris pushed his door open, rounded the car to the other side and offered a hand to help her out.

"Thanks."

They walked the few steps to her doorstep and faced each other. Their gazes met and locked for several silent moments. Chris leaned forward. His kiss was like the brush of a feather. Despite the softness, electrifying currents shot through Serenity, igniting a hunger. She reached a hand behind his back and pulled him to her.

He slid his arms around her back and kissed her deeper. "You know what I like about you?"

"What?"

"You seem so unfazed by your own beauty."

She blushed. "Thanks—I guess. Was that a compliment?"

Chris nodded. She giggled, still flush from his comment. He swallowed her laugh with another kiss. Immediately, those flashes of electricity returned. Chris kissed her like he'd never let go. She certainly didn't want him to. She held on tighter. He pulled her closer. They kissed, breathed, reconnected and continued that pattern. Despite the coolness of the spring night's air, warmth rose in her. Lost in the kiss, she'd temporarily forgotten where she was. The instinctive moan rising in her throat pulled her back into reality. She ended the kiss to catch her breath. Arching her back exposed her neck. Chris planted a trail of kisses there.

"Come inside," she whispered.

"Serenity." His voice was low and husky.

She put her finger across his lips. "I want you to come

inside." She knew what she was asking. The promise indicated by the way he kissed her was the catalyst for her boldness.

"Are you sure?"

Serenity returned a breathless "Yes."

He kissed her one more passionate time, generating an elevated level of heat between them. She fumbled with the keys, slipped them into the lock and swung the door open. Without parting, they walked through the door, connected by a kiss. She kicked the door closed and turned the lock.

A wave of urgent passion shot through her. A hungry need compelled her. Serenity tugged at his jeans. In haste he fumbled with his belt until his pants slipped down to his ankles. She pushed his shirt up, exposing his taut chest. She kissed his nipples. Chris pulled the shirt over his head and tossed it. Bare-chested, he drew her closer, removed her shirt and swiftly unclipped her bra. She pressed her exposed breasts against his torso. His rigid erection strained against her stomach. Their skin was hot to the touch.

Serenity groaned in anticipation. Chris unbuckled her jeans and shimmied them past her rounded hips. She removed her mouth from the sweet savor of his lips and looked around.

"Over there." She pointed to the dining table.

He stepped out of his dangling pants and placed his foot on the seat of hers so she could remove them, as well. He lifted her up and she wrapped her legs around his back. Moisture pooled at her center as he carried her to the table and laid her down. He moved a chair aside to give them clearance before turning his full attention back on Serenity. For a moment, he just stared into her eyes as she lay with her back against the teak wood. His smile spoke of his appreciation. He touched her as if he were handling a precious work of art, fingering her lips, neck, breasts and navel with gentle caresses. His lips explored the same path hers had on him the moment before. Serenity squirmed under the blazing trail he'd left against her skin. She moaned again.

"Are you sure?" Chris asked.

Serenity nodded her head. She knew what she was doing, and she knew what she wanted.

"Wait here." After another peck on her swollen lips, Chris left her there for a quick moment in search of his pants. Digging in his pockets, he retrieved a square foil package and returned to her.

Her loins pulsated in anticipation of him. He tasted her. Serenity's breath caught when his tongue flicked across her bud. He learned her quickly, responding most to the gestures that produced hisses, groans and gasps, repeating them until a sharp orgasm ripped through her, rendering her immobile for a moment. He lapped at the juices flowing from her until she was too tender to stand his touch any longer. Seconds later, she wiggled from his gasp, panting and convulsing. She pushed him away. Immediately he sheathed himself and entered her. The walls of her womanhood clenched around him. He released a guttural grunt.

He started with a deliberate grind, maneuvering himself in circular motions, the pleasure so intense she thought she'd burst into thousands of tiny pieces. She grasped at the table. Her body reacted of its own volition. She milked his erection with a snug grip, matching his motions. He groaned, increasing his tempo a notch. Leaning forward, he pressed his chest against hers and nibbled on her lips as he drove himself inside her in long, deep measures. She threw her arms around him, and her touch must have taken him higher.

Chris pumped with a new level of urgency. Serenity panted and squeezed him tighter. He applied a distinct groan to each thrust, which grew louder and longer until they strung together like one long guttural note.

"Oh," Serenity chanted over and over again.

Chris called her name. Her "ohs" turned to "ahs," adding harmony to their erotic song—a crescendo of ecstasy led them to the edge of sanity. Temporarily blinded by the intense pleasure, Serenity saw white flashes of light. Her body trembled as she gushed a blissful release. Chris bucked wildly and then pushed himself inside as far as he could manage. Body spasms arrested his mobility as life emptied from him. He shuddered and collapsed on top of her, breathing as if he'd finished a marathon. She wrapped her arms around him tighter. A few random tremors flowed through him. He kissed her molten skin until their heart rates descended to a normal pace.

He picked her limp body up and carried her to the bed. She lay curled in his arms with her back to his protective chest. She was glad she'd given him a second chance and couldn't imagine being in a better place.

## Chapter 20

"What did you do to me?" Chris tried to sound serious.

"What do you mean?" It worked. Serenity seemed alarmed.

"I think you put something on me." He laughed. Hearing her voice on the phone made him wish he could see her face.

"Oh!" Serenity sucked her teeth. "Silly. You made me nervous. I should ask you the same thing. I didn't want you to leave last night, even though I was still exhausted from not getting any sleep the night before. I'm going to have to ration myself with you." He heard her yawn.

"Don't start that."

"I'm sorry, but I'm tired, and it's all your fault. What time did you even leave last night?"

"You mean this morning."

"Well, yeah. I guess." She chuckled. The sound was like a warm caress to his ear.

"I have to be honest with you. I have never, ever—" he stressed "—stayed over at a woman's house two nights in a row for any reason. This whole thing has me..." Chris stopped abruptly. His emotions confounded him. The things he wanted to say had to be conveyed in person.

"What?"

"We'll talk about that later."

"You're being mysterious again, Mr. Chandler?"

Chris chuckled. "I called to ask about your schedule tonight. I want to take you somewhere."

"I have a meeting with my board. We should be done around eight. Why? What's up?"

"How about I pick you up at eight thirty?"

"Sure. Are you going to give me more information?"

"Of course not!" He laughed, imagining those pretty lips of hers fashioned into a defiant pout. "I've gotta run. See you tonight?"

"I guess."

"Ha! You'll know soon enough. Oh, and check your social media profiles. Good day, my lady."

"Okay, Mr. Chandler. See you later."

"Eight thirty," he confirmed.

"Enjoy your day," Serenity said before ending the call.

It was those simple gestures that enticed Chris, drawing him to her hard and fast. Something as simple as bidding him an enjoyable day held so much substance. He couldn't remember any of the women he'd dated offering caring sentiments so naturally. It reminded him of what seemed to be missing from his generation's interactions. His parents shared these sweet exchanges all the time. He realized then that he wanted what his parents had, and it hadn't seemed possible until now. She'd awakened him to a new reality. He actually wanted her to enjoy her day too, to know how her day went or to find out how she was feeling. Chris vowed to make sure he did the same going forward. This was new, but he liked it.

Chris pulled into the lot at his family's company, shut

off the engine and sauntered into the building. Starting his mornings with Serenity set his days in motion the right way.

"Good morning, Chris. You're looking awfully chipper today," Clarissa, the receptionist, said. They'd managed respectfully playful interactions since she'd first started a few months back. "In fact, you've been rather chipper for a couple of weeks now." She tilted her head and looked at him skeptically. "What's her name? I bet she's really pretty. Is it someone here?"

"Ha!" Chris shook his head. "Bye, Clarissa." He continued inside the office.

"You'll spill the details sooner or later. Maybe I'll meet her when she comes to meet you for lunch one day," she continued to his retreating back.

He could hear her giggling even after the door was closed. Chris knew she was being more than inquisitive. Clarissa had been enamored with him from the start. She'd never crossed any inappropriate boundaries, and he'd made sure to never send her any mixed signals. His days of sleeping with staff had ended a while ago. He'd matured upon reaching the side of his twenties that rounded closer to the thirties.

He'd also learned a very valuable lesson about mixing business with scandalous pleasure after an in-office affair had turned messy. A starry-eyed admin he'd been bedding had mistaken their intense trysts for love. She'd lost it one day when another woman he'd been seeing showed up for a surprise lunch. Casey had acted out so badly that his father ended up firing her on the spot. He was furious at Chris for messing around with other employees and promised that if it ever happened again that Chris would be the one without a job. Chris took his father seriously and, from that point on, he hardly made eye contact with female employees—especially new ones.

He headed to his office, removed his suit jacket and tossed it over the back of his chair. He walked to the windowed wall and looked out over the winding walking path flanked by lush greenery. Employees often enjoyed their lunch on the benches placed along the path. He focused on the footbridge reaching over the Japanese pond. He often took to a bench to think critically about strategies, like the one he and his sister needed to come up with to maintain sustainability during the closing of the major supermarket chain.

He thought about strolling along that path now to work out his feelings. He was half kidding when he asked Serenity about what she'd done to him. Never had he felt so sure about a woman in his life, and never had he been so confused by his feelings. He'd told her that time didn't matter, but it did. How could he feel so strongly about a woman in such little time? Especially after meeting her in the one way he thought he'd never find a woman—online.

Chloe and Donovan's relationship had moved fast, but they'd known each other for decades. Chris hadn't known Serenity for three full months but felt like he knew her before he'd met her. She was that woman he'd imagined but wasn't sure existed—the one who defied the hollow, superficial options he thought he'd end up settling for. He couldn't see himself letting that go.

He thought about getting Kent and Ray on the phone but turned on his heel and started toward his father's office, quickly covering the distance to the opposite end of the floor.

Three quick raps got his father's attention. Bobby Dale spun in his office chair to face Chris. With the desk phone propped between his ear and shoulder, he held up one finger and then waved Chris in. Scratching a note across a sticky pad, Bobby Dale ripped it off and stuck it below the keyboard on his laptop. A moment later, he ended the call after a hearty laugh and promised to put a meeting on his calendar.

"What's up, son?" Bobby Dale focused on Chris sitting across from him.

"Hey, Pops. You have a minute?"

"Always got a minute for you. What's up?"

Chris took a deep breath, gathering his thoughts. "It's about Serenity."

His father sat back and lifted his chin. "Nice girl. What about her?"

Chris took a moment before speaking. "I'm not sure…" He paused, reframing his comment. "When you feel a certain way about a woman, should it matter how long you've known one another?"

The older man raised both brows, leaned forward and smiled. "You like this woman, huh?"

"I do. I already know that she's nothing like anyone I've ever dated."

"That's usually an indication. I felt that way about your mother when I met her."

"How did you know she was the right one?"

Bobby Dale reared back and chuckled. "I just knew I couldn't see myself without her."

"But we haven't been seeing each other for long at all."

Bobby Dale tilted his head. "Son, time doesn't dictate what you feel."

Chris absorbed his father's statement, letting it seep past the notion that time mattered. In fact, he was willing to remove time as a factor altogether and allow the magnetism that drew him in to take the lead. He was going to take the pressure off himself, enjoy Serenity's company and see what happened.

"Thanks." Chris stood with a renewed sense of purpose.

Back in his office, he jumped on the phone with Kent and Ray to confirm plans for later in the day. An area of the kitchen in the wine bar was still under renovation due to the fire. They had come a long way in a short period of time. Fortunately, the fire had been a small one, and business had only been affected for a few days before they were able to begin working around the damaged area.

"We need to meet at the bar to go through some paperwork with our insurance guy. He said he could be there today at six," Kent said.

This would affect Chris's prep plans for Serenity tonight, but he had to handle business. "Okay. Any idea how long it will take?"

"He didn't say. I'm hoping it won't be long. We still have to get ready for the crowd later," Ray added.

"I know, and I wanted to pick Serenity up. I may have to have her meet me there."

"Oh, yeah!" Kent said. Chris imagined him rubbing the palms of his hands together, based on the way he sounded. "I can't wait to officially meet her. Seeing her sprint through the gala last weekend didn't count."

"What a way for her to find out. You're lucky she answered your calls after that," Ray said.

"I'm still trying to figure out how it happened. That was a hell of a coincidence," Kent said.

"A coworker invited her because her boyfriend had some kind of work emergency."

"That should be a lesson for all of us. This world is way too small for fake online identities!" Ray's laughter barreled through the phone line.

"Ha!" Kent cosigned. "Speaking of online…I guess you've officially changed your perspective on online dating, huh?"

"Whatever!" Chris said, dismissing their digs. "Serenity is a good woman. I'll admit I never expected to meet someone like her."

Chris was the target of their teasing this time around. He took it well since he was often dishing it.

A shadow caught Chris's attention. He looked up to find Jewel standing in his office door.

"I'll catch up with you later. There's some business I need to handle here."

"Cool." That was Ray's version of goodbye.

"Don't forget. Six o'clock," Kent said.

"Six o'clock," Chris and Ray repeated.

By the time Chris ended the call, Jewel was standing at his desk with an armful of files.

"I have news." Jewel dropped the files on the desktop. "Another major retailer is closing. Dad wants our preliminary plan by morning, showing how we'll attempt to minimize the impact on business."

Chris sat back and huffed. One way or another, he was going to get to Serenity tonight.

# *Chapter 21*

Despite being exhausted, Serenity still looked forward to seeing Chris. He'd become her respite. Spending time with him made her feel like she was pampering herself. Right now she needed to lavish herself with all the special attention she could obtain. As much as she loved teaching, her new schedule offered few breaks, and she was starting to feel the strain. The lessons she gave outside of work and planning for the gala swallowed any downtime she could have enjoyed. And the meeting with the board hadn't lifted her spirits. Sponsorships and ticket sales were down from the previous year, despite doing all they could. As she drove home, all of these thoughts whirled in her mind.

The one bright spot in her life, besides Chris, was the letter she had received from the Chandler Foundation. Her grant had been approved. After receiving the letter, Serenity had called Jade to say thank-you. Jade had made it clear that the funding had been approved because the foundation valued the work that Heartstrings was doing, and the fact that Serenity was dating her brother had no bearing on their decision. Happily, she reached out to her contacts in Brazil and was now awaiting their response about when they would like to start the program. Even though her school year would end in several weeks, in South America they were approaching the middle of their school year. Since she hadn't heard from her contacts yet, she assumed they'd want to start the program early next year when their new term began.

At eight on the dot, Chris called.

"Hey there, Mr. Chandler." She spoke through the Bluetooth system in her car.

"How's it going, beautiful?"

"On an amazing note, I got the grant for the program in South America, but I figured you probably knew that." Serenity mustered up the strength to squeal.

"Congratulations! Jade did mention it but, as a board member, I don't usually get involved in the day-to-day operations of the foundation business. She handles all of that."

"I'm so excited but totally exhausted."

"Sounds like your day was like mine. Tell me about it."

Serenity unloaded the toils of the past twelve hours on Chris, who listened attentively. She had to admit that it felt great to vent.

"I hope you're not too tired for tonight. We have to celebrate, but it sounds like kicking back is just what you need after such a long day."

"I'll be just fine, Chris."

"Will you still be ready by eight thirty?"

"Can we make it nine?"

"That won't be a problem. Your driver will be waiting."

"My driver? Chris—"

"See you later, beautiful."

"Chris," she said again and heard him chuckle. "Fine.

See you later," she added, abandoning her attempt to get him to reveal more information. It never worked anyway.

When Serenity hung up with him, she dialed her mom. "Hey, lady." She paused. "Why are you breathing hard?"

"I'm running," Avis Williams said.

"From who?" Serenity couldn't help her outburst. She leaned toward the steering wheel from laughing so hard.

"Silly! I'm with your dad."

"He's running too?"

"I wish. At least he's out here with me."

"Wow! I'm so proud of both of you."

"I think he got jealous of all the weight we lost. He's trying to get in on the action."

"That's good. Want me to call you back?"

"Talk to me. I can run and listen at the same time."

"I met somebody."

"Wait!" The phone went silent for a moment. "Now say that again," her mother said, panting.

"I met someone."

"That's what I thought you said. Details!"

"I didn't mention anything at first because I wasn't sure if he'd be around long because we met—" Serenity wasn't sure how her mother would respond "—online."

"Online! You?"

"Yeah, I know. But, Mom, he's charming, considerate—gorgeous. I've even met his family, his parents and sisters." Serenity kept the fact that he was a Chandler and that he owned a wine bar to herself for now. She told her mother about how quickly their relationship had progressed.

"When do I get to meet him?"

"Soon, Mom. I've been so busy."

"I know, honey. With school, Heartstrings, the gala, lessons…"

"I'm so glad you understand, Ma."

"I used to be such a busy lady too. Just don't burn yourself out. I miss you."

"I miss you too."

"Okay. Let me get back to running. I'm looking forward to checking this dude out."

"Soon enough."

"Bye, sweetie."

Serenity blew a kiss to her mom before hanging up, then pulled into her parking spot. She had just enough time for a quick turnaround. She didn't even bother taking the mail from the box as she passed it. Inside her apartment, she dropped her bag near the door, kicked off her shoes and headed straight for the shower. Standing under the hot spray, she closed her eyes and allowed the pulsing water to knead the stress from her muscles. Feeling refreshed, she anointed her body with peppermint body butter. The aroma invigorated her.

She searched her closet for something to wear. Chris hadn't given her any information, so she had no idea how to dress. Sliding hangers aside, she spotted a black strapless romper. She pulled it out, looked it over and noticed the tags were still attached. She remembered that it had been too tight when she'd first brought it home. She groaned and almost put it back in the closet. "Let's just see," she said aloud, turning to her full-length mirror. Serenity held the romper up to her body and sighed.

"What the heck." She stepped into the garment. "Come on, now. Be nice and fit." She glided the romper past her curves with ease. "It fits!" she squealed. Turning to the side, she admired the outfit. Her brilliant smile gleamed in the mirror. She felt even better than she had after the shower.

The doorbell rang at the same time as her phone. Picking up the cell, she trotted to the door.

"Hey, you."

"Are you ready, beautiful?" The sounds of Chris's deep voice seeped to her core, awakening that spark that only he had been able to stir.

Serenity looked out the window, spotting a limousine and the shadow of a body at her door.

"The driver's here? I can't believe it's nine o'clock already! I need two more minutes."

"I'll tell him that you'll be right out."

"Thanks. See you soon."

Excitement raced through her like an electric current. She'd all but forgotten how tired she was. Jogging back to her room, she pulled a tapered jacket from the closet, stuck a pair of dangling earrings in her ears and slipped her feet into a pair of low comfortable pumps. Her outfit was casual enough for a relaxed atmosphere and chic enough for something more upscale. Snatching her purse on her way out the room, she made her way outside. The driver was waiting for her at the door. He escorted her to the car, opened the door and made sure she was settled before taking the driver's seat.

It had been years since Serenity had ridden in a limo. She looked around at the lights running along the ceiling, ran her hand along the fine leather seats and then spotted a white box. Upon closer inspection, she saw that her name was written on it. She opened the package to find an arrangement of exotic chocolates and a card that read *delectable and rare, just like you*. She held the card to her chest and shook her head. That Chris sure did know how to make a girl blush. One by one, she picked up each piece and inhaled its aroma. They smelled so sweet. Serenity already knew this was going to be the perfect way to end her evening. She'd be tired tomorrow when she arrived at school, but the struggle would be well worth it. Nestling into the seat, she laid the chocolates across her lap and took in the scenery flitting by the window.

A while later, the vehicle pulled to a stop. The driver opened her door and helped her out. Serenity stood, taking notice of the trendy block with coffeehouses, restaurants and shops. They were parked in front of a place with a black awning with the words *The Reserve* written in crimson. Several patrons sat in the cool breeze at the café tables sprinkled along the sidewalk.

"You're just in time." Chris met her at the entrance with two other men. "Serenity, meet my friends and business partners, Kent and Ray. Welcome."

"Hello, gentlemen. Nice to meet you."

"Pleasure to meet you too, Serenity." Kent shook her hand.

"Nice seeing you again," Ray said.

"I'm sorry. We've met?"

"Not officially. We were at the gala with Chris last week. We mostly saw the back of your head."

Serenity's hand flew to her mouth. "I'm sorry."

"No need to be embarrassed," Kent said with a smile. "I'm glad to meet you on much better terms."

"Oh, believe me, the pleasure is ours. We finally have someone to take Chris off our hands," Ray teased.

Chris chuckled and led her to a seat near a stage set up for a band. She scanned the space, admiring the contemporary decor. One entire wall held bottles of wine behind glass casings.

"Will the band play tonight?" Serenity asked as she sat down.

"Just for you. Now, what do you feel like having?" Chris asked, then nodded at a short blonde, who walked over and handed her a menu. Chris sat across from Serenity.

"What do you recommend?"

"We have an amazing Pinot Noir. You could pair that with our choice cheese, chocolate and cracker platter. The duck or veggie flatbreads are pretty popular. We also have delicious salads and sliders—veggie, mushroom, turkey or beef. You pick."

"So much of this menu sounds tasty. I think I'll go for the…" Serenity looked up and down the menu once more. "Okay, I'll take the Pinot Noir and the duck flatbread."

"Excellent choice." Chris looked into her eyes and held her gaze a moment. Serenity's cheeks felt flush once again. "You look beautiful tonight. I hope you enjoy yourself."

"I can already tell that tonight is going to be great."

He kissed the back of her hand. "I hope so." Serenity heard some rumbling. Chris smiled.

"Hi, Serenity." It was a trio.

Serenity looked up, and her eyes met with Chris's sister Chloe. Right behind her stood Jewel and Jade.

"Hi, ladies." Standing, she embraced each sister.

Jade and Jewel joined her at the table. Chloe remained standing. The friend that Chris had introduced as Ray introduced a pretty girl as his fiancée, Brynn. Another round of greetings circulated as Brynn joined them at the table.

Kent took the small stage where the instruments were set up and welcomed everyone. "We've got something special in store for tonight. Are you ready?"

"Woo!" a few patrons yelled. Some clapped. First I'd like to call Chris's big sister Chloe to the stage."

Just then, a tall gentleman stepped up and kissed Chloe with an affection so sweet it made Serenity blush. He also joined them at their table. Jewel and Jade stood and hugged him before introducing him to Serenity as Chloe's fiancé, Donovan Rivers.

Chloe took the stage and absorbed the entire crowd's attention. One or two random requests were shouted from the audience. Chloe smiled and winked, not making any promises.

The band fell in place behind her. She consulted with the keyboard player for a brief moment. He nodded to the other players, and the drummer tapped four beats before they all joined in. Chloe began singing a jazzy ballad, mesmerizing the audience, including Serenity and, especially, Donovan.

After her next song, Chloe returned to their table, waving at the adoring crowd. Donovan pulled Chloe into a tight embrace and kissed her as if they were alone in the room. Serenity smiled and looked away, feeling like she was intruding on their intimate moment. Donovan seemed to be pretty smitten by Chloe. He held her hand even though they sat right next to each other. Serenity admired the careful attention they paid to one another. She believed she could have that with Chris. He was so considerate and attentive to her.

Serenity cast her eyes toward the ceiling. What was she doing? She and Chris were just starting out. Who knew what the future held? Though she had every intention of finding out, she wanted to be cool about it. If it worked out well, that would be wonderful. If not, she would always enjoy the time she'd spent getting to know him. If this was meant to be, it would happen, she told herself.

Serenity was catapulted from the recesses of her private thoughts when she heard Chris call her name. He was onstage, encouraging her to join him. Serenity looked around as everyone clapped. Chloe urged her to go. Serenity took a sip of her wine, put her napkin aside and stood. Applause erupted. She shook her head at Chris and smiled.

Onstage, Chris took her hand. "We're going to play together." His slick smile alerted her to the fact that his pun spoke of more than just the instruments.

Serenity giggled. No stranger to playing before crowds, she still felt the adrenaline course through her veins.

"Pick your instrument," Chris told her.

She looked at the keyboard and pointed. Chris approved with a wink. Serenity sat behind it and tinkered with the keys. "So, what are we going to play, Mr. Chandler?"

Chris tilted his head toward Ray, who drummed an intro. With his sax, Chris laid his melody over the instrumental version of a popular soul song about lovers getting to know each other. Serenity bobbed to the drumbeat, smiling her admiration of Chris's musical skills. He had the sax matching every nuance of the lyrics. Still swaying, she began strumming keys, artfully filling the room with harmony.

Moving and playing, she tucked her bottom lip into her mouth and allowed the music to carry her away. The room ceased to exist, leaving only the pulse of the drumbeat behind. It was just Chris and her. He faced her, blowing notes with his eyes connected to her soul. She felt him inside her heartbeat, making her feel sexy. The rhythm became sultry. She looked down at the piano keys momentarily and set her eyes back on Chris. He winked at her. The womanly parts of her awakened. They teased each other with notes and riffs, sensually caressing one another with the music they created.

The song ended but their sultry connection continued.

Serenity stood, and Chris put the sax aside. The audience was on their feet, whooping, clapping, cheering. Their gazes remained linked. Serenity sauntered over to Chris. It felt like she floated. He pulled her into his arms and kissed her lips. Taking her hand, they faced the audience and bowed. She could feel the quickening of his pulse in their hands. Still caught up in the exhilarating effects of the music they had created together, she became aware of the rhythm of her own heartbeat. That was the most fun she'd ever had performing in front of a crowd. She wanted to walk off the stage and go straight home to lie in Chris's arms.

Being in a public place, she maintained her poise. At the crowd's request, they played a few more songs together. When she returned to the table, Chris's sisters praised her talent. For the next hour, they drank wine, nibbled on cheese and flatbreads, and laughed.

One by one, the guests departed until it was just Donovan, Kent, Ray, Brynn and Chris's sisters at the table. Chloe and Donovan were the next to leave, followed by Jewel and Jade. Serenity and Brynn chatted while the guys closed up shop. Serenity really liked Brynn and was surprised to find out that she and Ray also had met through an online dating site. She could see the two of them becoming friends.

Finally, the men came out from the back, and they all left together, with Chris locking up for the night. Saying their goodbyes, Chris walked with Serenity to his car, parked a few feet away from the front of the wine bar.

He opened the passenger door for her to enter and paused. Stepping close enough for Serenity to feel his breath, Chris lifted Serenity's chin and kissed her lips again.

"Can I take you home?"

"Sure you can, silly. How else will I get there?"

"Not your home." Chris narrowed his gaze. His penetrating stare caused her breath to catch. "Mine."

"I'd love to go home with you, Mr. Chandler."

He kissed her one more time, made sure she was settled in and drove home with an urgency that followed them inside the house, causing them to leave a trail of clothes from the door.

A blinding hunger swept over Serenity. Her skin grew hot. Chris matched her intensity kiss for kiss and caress for caress. They groped each other as if survival required their touch. Considering it was her first time visiting his home, she hardly noticed how spacious the house was. Serenity did recall the massive walk-in shower, where they made love on the floor under the pulsing jets, spraying from the nozzles in the walls. She remembered grabbing handfuls of the soft luxury linens lining his California king-size bed when their rendezvous moved from the bathroom to the bedroom. And she remembered waking to the heat of his tongue as he tasted her essence once more before dawn. Serenity didn't know if she'd ever get enough of Christian Chandler.

## Chapter 22

Once again, Chris couldn't wait to get home. He'd left Serenity in his bed to do an early-morning local television interview with Kent and Ray about the rising popularity of *The Reserve*. He would have brought her with him but knew she needed rest after her busy week and their rambunctious night together.

Chris planned to spend the rest of his Saturday with her. Over the past few weeks, their increasingly busy schedules afforded them few opportunities to spend time together. Most nights, however, they slept in each other's arms, only to get up early and start all over again—bidding each other great days until they came together again late at night. Eventually, they started choosing a day during the weekend to spend together from morning till night. Today, they hadn't made concrete plans. Staying in bed the entire time had crossed his mind, but he would consult with Serenity to see if there was anything she wanted to do.

He wheeled the car into his two-car garage and pressed the remote to close the door behind him. He moved with urgency, craving her presence. Chris entered his home, stepped out of his shoes at the door and called out to Serenity. He even liked the way her name felt on his tongue. She'd become just that to him—serenity. With all that was going on in his life—the family business, the frenzy created by the popularity of The Reserve—Chris needed a slice of peace. Serenity had become his tranquility. He worried about nothing when they were together.

"Babe!" Chris peeked into several rooms as he moved about in search of her. He called her again just before noticing that she was curled up on the love seat in the family room. The sight of her beautiful face while she slept peacefully made him pause. For moments, he simply watched the rise and fall of her torso. He desired to caress her cheek but didn't want to wake her. Picking up the remote, he aimed it at the television, shutting it off. She stirred at the sudden absence of sound.

Sitting on the arm of the chair, he listened to the rhythm of her breathing. As soft as it was, the sound was prominent against the quiet backdrop of his spacious home. He had purchased the house two years before, as an investment. It was an immediate bachelor pad until he and his friends had opened the wine bar. He began spending less time at his apartment in Manhattan. Now the house remained empty most of the time with his constant coming and going. One day, he'd have a wife and children to share it with. The family room would finally live up to its name.

Serenity stirred once more. Could she be the mother of his kids? Chris laughed at himself for even having those thoughts. They'd only been dating exclusively for several months. *Exclusive.* Chris tilted his head. They'd never actually defined what they were doing. He wasn't seeing anyone else and assumed she wasn't either, since every minute they weren't together was accounted for. Through the week, they took turns sleeping at each other's homes, rarely spending their nights alone anymore. Things had progressed quickly, yet he felt like they were exactly where they were supposed to be with each other.

Serenity's eyes fluttered open, and that brought a smile to Chris's face.

"Hey." She cleared her throat.

"You finally got some rest, I see. I didn't want to wake you."

She looked thankful. "How was the interview?" Her voice was a drowsy whisper.

"Fun, actually." He sat on the couch next to her. She rose to clear a space for him. "You know how it is when Ray, Kent and I get together." He turned the television back on, set it to a music channel and lowered the volume.

"I could imagine." Serenity covered her yawn.

Chris locked his gaze on her and pondered a question. "Is this moving fast for you?"

She sat up straighter. "You mean 'us.'" She pointed to each of them. He nodded. "Sometimes I think so, but it doesn't actually feel that way."

He was glad she felt the same sense of familiarity. "Why do you think that is?"

She took a deep breath and let it out slowly. "I've wondered myself. Maybe it's because we spent so much time in the beginning just getting to know each other. We shared so much. By the time I finally met you, I felt like I already knew you." Serenity paused. "Well, I thought I knew Chris Mullins."

Chris lifted his chin and narrowed his eyes. Serenity giggled. "That's not fair."

"You bamboozled me, Mr. Chandler."

"I had to make sure you wasn't a mad woman!" His

laugh filled the room, drowning out the music playing in the background.

"Chris!" Serenity scolded and tossed the throw pillow she'd been sleeping on at him. "I should have used a fake name. You could have been crazy too."

Chris studied her when their laughter died down. "I still can't believe I met you online."

Serenity gave him a pensive gaze. "Why?"

"Because you're perfect," Chris said unwaveringly and stood to put the remote on the ottoman. Serenity's mouth was ajar when he turned to sit back down.

"Perfect?" she said softly. "You think I'm perfect?"

"For me you are. You know the story. I was trying to get away from the same kind of person. I was sick of comparing résumés and pedigrees. You're more than that. More than I expected, and I like it—a lot!"

"Aww, Chris!" Serenity hopped into his lap and kissed him all over the face.

Chris shook his head and grinned.

"Well, I like you a lot too. You're considerate, charming, family-oriented and pretty darn cute." Serenity kissed his nose.

"I am a pretty good catch," Chris teased.

"I should have added *arrogant*, huh?"

"I'm glad you're the one who caught me." Chris kissed her blushing cheeks and contemplated his next statement. "I've thought about how time should be considered when it comes to us, but that no longer matters. I just know that I want to be with you."

Serenity's hands flew to her mouth, and then she threw them around his neck. Her response was an impassioned kiss. Her phone rang, interrupting their tender moment. They released each other and she looked down at her phone on the floor near the love seat. She hesitated a moment but answered, flashing a wide apologetic smile and then a pout.

"Hey, Mom…Nothing, for a change…Yes." Serenity looked over at Chris. "When?" Chris kissed the crook of her neck and nibbled on her ear. "Okay…" Serenity's breath caught. "Of course." Chris's hand covered her breast. Gently, he squeezed one and then the other. "Okay, Mom. I'll see you later. I've got to go."

Chris snickered. He enjoyed teasing her while she chatted with her mother. Serenity ended the call, laid the phone on the floor and lifted her neck, giving Chris greater access. He nuzzled closer, knowing that kissing her there made her weak with pleasure. She melted into his arms, and he desired her even more.

"Chris." She was breathless. His groan was his answer. "My mother would like us to come over for dinner. Are you ready to meet her?"

Chris pulled himself from the warmth of her neck and gazed directly into her eyes. Desire heated his core. "Dinner sounds great, but I want to start with dessert."

Serenity giggled. He captured her lips and laid her back on the couch. Carefully, he lifted her shirt, unsnapped her bra and freed her full breasts. He took turns taking her pebbled nipples into his mouth. He shimmied her pants past her hips and planted a trail of kisses along her inner thigh until he reached her warm, waiting center. Parting those lips, he feasted on her until she screamed his name and scampered from his grasp.

Hearing his name through her passionate cries triggered another level of heat inside of Chris. Urgency took hold of him. Covering his erection, he entered her warm canal, driving himself deep with long, rhythmic strides. Serenity moaned her delight—the sounds elevating with the heightening intensity. The cushioned heat of her suctioned him. He hissed and found himself grunting with each stroke. He pushed as far as he could go and held on. She milked him with orgasmic spasms. He lost the ability to regulate his pace, his body curled forward hard, and he bucked, pounding into her. His release was so powerful it crippled him, leaving him immobile for several moments. His eyes rolled upward as he completely gave in to the incredible pleasure. Serenity wrapped her legs around him and held him tight as they reached their peaks in unison.

Chris had to wait to regain mobility in order to speak. "Now I'm ready for dinner."

# Chapter 23

Serenity was sure her parents would be fond of Chris's attractive personality but couldn't help fidgeting. He squeezed her hand gently and placed a soft kiss on the back of it. That put her at ease. Her mother was already excited to meet him. Avis Williams was naturally inquisitive, but Curtis was likely to interrogate Chris as if he'd just hauled him into the local precinct for a major crime.

"Stop worrying. Your parents are going to love me." Chris chuckled.

Serenity shook her head and laughed. "Because of your *confidence*, Mr. Chandler?"

"Wrong *c* word. Charming is what I was going for."

"I'll admit it. You are quite charming."

At the light, Chris leaned over and puckered. Serenity stretched her body over the wide console separating them in his oversize SUV to meet him halfway. She kissed him through her smile. An impatient driver's blaring horn alerted them to the changed light.

Chris politely held his hand up acknowledging the delay. "If I recall correctly, your dad likes sports, right?" He turned to Serenity as he eased into the intersection.

"He's a huge football fan."

"Okay. And he's a retired police officer?"

"You remembered." Serenity beamed. "I'm impressed. He was a lieutenant when he left the force."

"I pay attention."

"I see that."

"And your mom is a teacher."

"She taught for a few years and became a high-school guidance counselor." Serenity appreciated his questions.

"Got it. Any hobbies I should know about?"

"Dad loves his grill. Mom jokes that he prefers it to her sometimes. Mom's new hobby is working out. We used to do it together all the time, but my schedule changed all that. We lost our first twenty-five pounds together when she found out that she was borderline diabetic. She's in great shape now and trying to get Dad on board. My father teases her about riding alongside her while she would run, like Rocky's trainer did in those old movies." She chuckled and turned her attention from Chris to the street. She noted they were two blocks away from the restaurant where they were meeting her parents for dinner. After a long inhale, she let the air out in a rush and prepared to see her dad.

Serenity's father, Curtis Williams, was protective. He never used the term *stepdad* and told Serenity when he married her mother that she was lucky to have two dads who loved her, even though she hadn't seen her biological father in years. Eventually, Curtis officially adopted her, giving her his last name.

Serenity noticed her father's van parked outside the restaurant. "Dad is overprotective and a master interrogator. So be ready."

"I would be too, if you were my daughter." Chris winked again. "It'll be fine."

"If you say so."

Chris pulled in behind the van. Serenity stayed inside the car until he came around to her side to open the door. Taking her by the hand, he gave her a reassuring squeeze as they walked into the restaurant together. It was her parents' favorite eatery, which they frequented weekly. She and Chris were on their turf.

Serenity spotted her mother waving and pointed them out to the hostess. Both were standing by the time she and Chris made it over to the table.

"Hey, sweetie!" Her mother embraced her, squeezing tight. She released Serenity, holding her at arms' length. "I've missed you. When are you coming back to spin class with me?"

"I can start back after the gala next week. With that and the wedding..." Serenity shook her head, not bothering to finish her sentence.

"Okay. I'll just have to wait."

"How's my baby girl?" Curtis held his burly arms open wide. Serenity stepped in, nuzzled her face into his broad chest and wrapped her arms around him.

"How's my big guy?"

Chuckling, Curtis's torso vibrated against his laugh. "Great, now that you're here." He kissed the top of her head.

"Mom. Dad." Serenity stepped out of his embrace. "This is..." She hesitated. Serenity hadn't introduced him before and wondered whether or not she should say *boyfriend*. At that moment, she realized that Chris hadn't officially met any of her family or friends. "...Christian Chandler. Chris, these are my amazing parents, Curtis and Avis Williams."

Chris and her dad exchanged a firm shake. "Pleasure to meet you, sir."

Curtis scrutinized Chris with narrowed eyes and a lifted chin. "I hope it's going to be a pleasure to meet you, as well."

Avis pursed her lips at Curtis. Serenity took a deep breath and held it. Her dad raised a brow and grinned. She released the breath she was holding.

"Serenity was sure to tell me how great you are. Any hero of hers is a hero of mine," Chris said.

Curtis's brilliant smile and swelled chest was a clear indication that Chris's comeback had had a positive effect.

"Hello, dear." Avis reached for Chris. "It's good to finally meet you."

"Serenity—" Chris pretended to look confused "—you didn't tell me you had a sister. I thought you were an only child." He kissed the back of Avis's hand.

Waving him off, Avis giggled. Chris smiled at Curtis, who lifted his brows and smiled back.

"Glad you were able to join us this evening," her dad said to both of them.

"Thank you for the invitation, sir."

Curtis gestured toward the waiting chairs. The men sat after making sure the women were seated. The waiter appeared with water, took drink orders and disappeared as unobtrusively as he had come.

"So, Christian."

"Please, sir. Call me Chris."

"Chris...what do you do for a living?"

*Dad's wasting no time at all.* Serenity felt like buckling her seat belt.

"I work the family business. We own a consumer-goods company and restaurant on the pier in Sag Harbor. I also run a wine bar with two buddies of mine."

"A savvy investor?" Curtis nodded, seemingly impressed. "Got a degree, son?"

"Yes, sir—with an MBA in business."

"Ivy League man?"

"Yes, sir," Chris said proudly.

"That's interesting."

"What goods?" Serenity's mother asked.

Chris provided a more thorough explanation.

"Oh my! I love those Mary Kate pies. Those things will get you in trouble." Avis chuckled.

"Mom learned how to curb her vicious sweet tooth."

"I didn't have much choice, but I'm feeling better than I have in years. But, just to let you know, we're sharing a dessert tonight." They all joined Avis in that laugh.

"So, young man, how did your family get into making baked goods?"

"It started with my grandparents. They moved here from a small town in South Carolina. Both were great cooks, and my grandmother, Mary Kate, came from a long line of skilled bakers. People loved her pies. They opened a small restaurant in Amityville. As a kid, my father and his siblings worked the restaurant. When he graduated with an MBA, he started focusing on ways to expand the business, and Chandler Food Corp. grew from there."

Curtis nodded. "And what exactly are your intentions with my daughter?"

Chris didn't seem to mind the questions Serenity's dad hurled his way. "It's been pleasantly surprising getting to know her. She's an amazing, smart and compassionate woman, and I'd love to see where this could go. I've never met a woman quite like Serenity."

Serenity couldn't help but blush. Both she and her mother were tuned into the men's conversation.

"Yes." A proud smile spread across Curtis's face. "She's quite special." He looked at Chris, and his expression turned serious. "Which is why you should know that I'm retired from law enforcement." Mr. Williams raised a brow.

"I know that, sir. You don't have to worry about me. I know a good woman when I see one, and I hold Serenity in the highest esteem." Chris flashed her an adoring smile. "I also know you're a huge sports fan." Curtis smiled. "Speaking of which, who were you rooting for this season?" Chris asked him.

"Man, those Knicks make me want to spit fire!"

Just like that, Chris had turned the conversation around. Curtis's passion for basketball unleashed itself for the next several minutes. Topics easily maneuvered from basketball to football, golf, smart investments and jazz greats. Before long, they were gabbing like old buddies.

Serenity loved the way Chris engaged her father. By the time they were done with dinner, her father laughed hard, slapped the table, pondered other perspectives and showed off his extensive knowledge of politics, music and history. Serenity's mother blushed, giggled and boasted about her new fit lifestyle. Her parents enjoyed talking about themselves. Chris learned as much about them as they learned about him. When dinner ended, the two couples headed to their respective cars.

"Come on by anytime, young man," Serenity's dad offered. "Perhaps we can meet on the course one of these days."

She was in awe. Never had her dad presented an open invitation to anyone she had dated.

Instead of going home, Serenity called Elisa and Rayne. The night ended with more cocktails, laughter and banter in Rayne and Ethan's newly renovated den.

Everyone who meant something to Serenity was smitten with Chris by midnight. By the time they fell asleep in each other's arms, her feelings for Chris had reached new heights.

# Chapter 24

Chris paced his small office at The Reserve. He huffed and dialed the number for the third time. There was still no answer. Kent and Ray were somewhere in the bar, handling business. He sat down and looked at his watch. There was still time. He hit the number again.

"Hello!"

Chris exhaled. "Hey, dude. Just checking in."

"No worries. I'm on my way."

"Great! See you there."

He placed the phone in his belt clip and went to search for Kent and Ray.

"I'm heading out now," he said to Ray, who was coming from the kitchen.

"Take pictures," Kent said to his back.

Chris turned around. "That's a good idea."

"Is Serenity coming back with you?" Ray asked.

"Yeah."

"Cool. Brynn asked. They really hit it off well."

Chris smiled. "That's a good thing—I think," he teased, and all three of them laughed.

Chris said his final goodbye and jumped into the car.

The surprise kept him smiling. What would Serenity say? What would the kids say?

Twenty minutes later, Chris pulled up in front of the center where Serenity was rehearsing with her young people in preparation for the gala that week. For several nights, they'd worked tirelessly to get ready for the performance. Now that they were down to their final hours, Chris wanted to reward all of them for the effort they had put in—Serenity included.

He had watched her give her all to her students, the kids at the center and her friend Rayne as they prepared for her wedding. Complaining wasn't her style, but he knew that Serenity was tired and even a bit overwhelmed. With all that she was doing for others, he wanted her to feel special.

He shut the engine and dialed the number one more time.

"I think I'm right around the corner," the voice said. "Yes. I'll be there in two minutes."

"Perfect." Chris exited the car and waited on the sidewalk.

Moments later, a silver Range Rover with out-of-state plates pulled behind him. Pride swelled in Chris's chest. He was glad to pull this off and could already anticipate the excitement that would erupt on the other side of the center's doors when they walked into the rehearsal unexpectedly.

"Glad to see you! Thanks for coming." Chris greeted his surprise guest by shaking his free hand.

"I told you. I'll do anything for the kids. Thanks for inviting me. Do they know I'm coming?"

"Nope." A Cheshire smile eased across Chris's lips.

"Even better. Let's make it happen."

Leading the way, Chris entered the center. At the reception desk, the woman's mouth dropped slightly. She recovered quickly enough.

"Good evening." He flashed a megawatt smile.

She cleared her throat. "Good evening. How can I help you?" She flipped her long hair behind her shoulder, offered a demure smile and looked back and forth between the two men.

"We're here for the Heartstrings rehearsal."

She turned down the coyness in her smile as she answered. "Sure. They practice down that hall to your right." She pointed long acrylic nails in that direction. Despite the soft pink of the polish, the pointed tips looked lethal. "They use the room all the way at the end."

"Thanks." Chris nodded politely.

"Have a great evening." Chris's guest tapped the desk, giving a polite nod, as well.

"I will now," she said under her breath.

The two headed down the hall, past the sounds of screeching sneakers and balls bouncing against hardwood floors in a small gym. Chris felt the adrenaline course through his veins, giving him a rush. As he drew closer to the room, the faint sounds of music grew in volume.

"Are you ready?" He turned back to ask his guest.

"Wait!" He opened his case and withdrew his instrument. Chris took hold of the case as the guest propped the violin on his shoulder. "Now," he said.

Chris turned the knob, slowly pushing the door open with a creak. Peeking in, he saw Serenity standing before her kids, conducting them, with her back to the door. He stepped in with his guest behind him.

"Yes!" Serenity encouraged them. "Pay attention, Chanel."

The youngster she'd addressed had stopped playing and stared with wide eyes past Chris.

Two others stopped playing, as well. Their widened eyes matched Chanel's, and their mouths dropped one by one.

"Guys. Come on! What—" Serenity turned to see what had caught their attention. Both hands flew to her open mouth.

Storm strummed the notes on his violin, continuing the song the kids seemed to have forgotten they were playing.

For a few seconds, they all seemed stuck in their surprise until one girl screamed, dropping her instrument. Jumping up and down, she yelled, "OMG! It's Storm Kensington! He's really here!"

Eating up their excitement, Storm continued playing, taking the remaining steps to where they practiced, in the rhythm he skillfully released into the atmosphere.

All the kids stood, giggling, covering their mouths or screaming. One girl put the back of her hand against her forehead and pretended to faint.

"Yo!" one young man said over and over.

"Chris!" Serenity found her voice. One hand covered her heart. She shook her head.

Chris could tell she was grateful.

Storm stopped playing, chuckling at the kids' response.

"No, don't stop!" The young man who had been chanting "yo" was bobbing to the beat.

"Then you'll have to join me. Let's go," Storm challenged him.

All of them scrambled for their instruments and played along with him. Serenity picked hers up and joined them too. Minutes later, they ended with a crescendo, laughing and still in awe that they'd just played with Storm Kensington.

After the last note, they dropped their instruments and ran over to Storm. Serenity ran over to Chris, wrapped her arms around him and kissed all over his face. They turned to the kids lavishing Storm with their attention and watched as he managed their explosive energy and excited outbursts in stride.

"Storm, can you play that new song from Champagne?" Chanel said to him.

"Yeah. Teach us that, please," another girl pleaded.

Chris and Serenity stood watching Storm interact with the kids. Serenity leaned against his side, under his arm. Still shaking her head, she sighed.

"Look at them. They're so excited."

Pride filled Chris's chest once again. "What about you?"

"I can't even describe how I feel right now. I know he said when we were at the concert that night that he would come by, but I just thought he was being nice. I never imagined he'd really come." She turned to face Chris. "Thank you."

Chris looked down into her face and noticed tears rolling. "Are you crying?"

Serenity pouted, staring up at him with puppy-dog eyes. Chris shook his head and both of them laughed.

"They are going to remember this for the rest of their lives." She stared back at them wistfully. "I'm never going to forget this." She turned to him again. "I can't thank the two of you enough, Chris."

He wanted to kiss her but decided to wait until they were alone. "I enjoy putting a smile on your face."

Her blush made the entire effort worthwhile.

Storm finished playing the song and applause erupted.

"Play another one."

"How about we play something together. What are you all working on for the gala?"

A gasp. "You know about the gala!" one of the kids said.

"I know a lot of things."

"Will you be there?" another kid asked.

"Perhaps."

"You should come. He can come, right, Ms. Serenity?"

"If he's available and in town, he can absolutely come."

"Yeah!" they yelled together.

For the next hour, Storm practiced with the kids, giving pointers on how to become a better player. He showed his versatility by playing other instruments. Chris hadn't thought beforehand about joining them but ran out to his car and retrieved his sax from the trunk. He often brought it to The Reserve with him, especially on nights that they hadn't booked any talent to play. He, Ray and Kent would take to the stage for jam sessions. Chris came back from the car and joined in, adding a jazzy flavor to their orchestra.

Chris would never have anticipated having so much fun playing with those kids and made a note to visit Serenity's rehearsals more. Now he truly understood her need to work with these kids and start her organization. Engaging with them triggered another side of him. Seeing their faces light up and the enthusiasm hit the roof made him want to hang with them more often. In that moment, he admired and desired her even more.

## Chapter 25

As if the stress of the day couldn't get any higher, Serenity received word from her contacts in Brazil. They wanted her to start the program right in the middle of their school year, requiring her to leave for South America immediately after her school let out for the summer. Her dream was coming true, but there was so much to be done before she could leave.

Her principal would need to find a music teacher to fill in for her by the time school started back. Surely he wasn't expecting her leave to begin so soon. Rayne would have to step up and do more to run the organization here at home. They might even need to hire someone else. Their operating budget was nearly nonexistent, so Serenity wondered how that would work out. And Chris... she was going to be away until December. She would come home for about two months during their summer break and would have to return for the next year for another four to five months. How would their relationship survive—if at all?

Serenity couldn't dwell on that. Heartstrings' gala would start in a few hours. Her mind needed to be on meeting Rayne at the gallery to set up. She'd taken the day off to get things in order.

Pushing past the speed limit, Serenity kept an eye out for state troopers. Her board members were coming to help set up, as well. Two of them were already at the venue when she arrived. Together, they emptied the back of Serenity's SUV, carrying loads of boxes inside. A while later, her mother and Rayne showed up. Elisa came a few minutes after that. Her mom worked with the caterers to set up the food and finalize the layout for serving the guests. The other board members arrived and set up the raffle prizes, items for the silent auction and a table where guests would check in. Everyone chipped in with decorations, covering the tables with rented red linens, centerpieces shaped like instruments, framed pictures of the kids they worked with and gift bags with chocolates molded into guitars, violins and pianos.

Within hours they transformed the place. The art adorning the walls created the perfect backdrop. Alberto, the owner of the gallery, had given Serenity the space for free. She thought back to the gala she attended with her coworker a few weeks back when she had discovered the truth about Chris. As swanky as that event had been, Serenity realized that she preferred the artsy charm of the gallery. It fit for now.

"What do we need to do now?" Elisa asked.

"Go home and get dressed," Serenity instructed. "I have my clothes with me. I can change in Alberto's office. I'll stick around here and make sure we didn't forget anything. Thank you all so much for your help."

"Yes," Rayne added, "we couldn't have done this without you. I'll be here with Serenity. See you all at five thirty."

Serenity's mom kissed her cheek. "Dad and I will be

back just before five. Make sure there's more than one copy of the guest list. Elisa and I will each need a list so we can get people checked in quickly."

"There should be at least three copies in the boxes under the check-in table."

"Okay, good. See you later, sweetie."

"Bye. Bye." Elisa kissed Serenity's and Rayne's cheeks before heading out.

When everyone had left, Serenity and Rayne sat down at one of the tables. Both women sighed.

"We did it, Serenity."

"Our second gala." She smiled. Serenity tilted her head and looked pensively at her friend. "How will you manage by yourself?"

"Pfft!" Rayne waved her hand dismissively. "Don't you worry. You've been doing most of the work since we started this. By the time you leave, the wedding will be over, and I will be able to dedicate much more time to the organization. You focus on those kids in Brazil. This is your dream."

"I know. I still can't believe it's happening. It was just a crazy idea when I first mentioned it to Darcy. The more we talked, the more we wanted to make it happen. Remember?"

"Yes, I remember. I'm still reeling over Darcy moving back to his village after being here and teaching at our school for so many years. That last trip he took really impacted him. And now the organization he started does so much for those kids. Adding music is going to be amazing."

"Dr. Stein is going to have a fit when I tell him I need to begin my leave of absence earlier."

"I know. But it'll work itself out." Rayne looked at her

watch. "Let's go through the checklist one more time, and then we can start getting dressed."

They looked up as the band was coming through the door.

"Right after we get them set up," Rayne said, standing.

"Welcome!" Serenity stood and walked over to greet the gentlemen carrying the equipment. They wore tuxedos and white shirts.

The lead singer, a woman, dressed elegantly in a black gown, said, "Great seeing you two again." After greetings and hugs, she asked, "Where would you like us to set up?"

"Right over here." Rayne waved her hand and led them to an area reserved for them on the side opposite the food.

One by one, the ladies went to freshen up and change. A while later, they emerged dressed in cherry red gowns, the company's colors. Serenity's shapely dress was set below her shoulders and opened at the bottom in a trumpet style. Rayne's strapless sweetheart top hugged at the waist and then flared into a full ball skirt that hid her silver shoes.

The two of them looked around, making sure everything was in place. Time moved at a quickened pace. Serenity's mother and father walked in. Avis looked stunning, her hair pulled into a neat bun perfectly set at the back of her head and wearing a strapless red jumpsuit with an extra piece of material that flared at the waist and flowed to the floor behind her. Curtis wore a black tux and bow tie and a cravat peeking out from his breast pocket.

Shortly after their arrival, the rest of her team came and prepared for the guests. The band created a backdrop of soothing tunes as guests mingled and drank cocktails. White-gloved catering staff passed around hors d'oeuvres on ivory porcelain platters among the intimate crowd of family, friends and coworkers. The director of the center arrived with Serenity's kids and their parents. She ran over to greet them, boasting of how wonderful they looked in their dressy clothes. She was so proud of them. She directed them to the back room with their instruments to prepare for their performance.

Serenity glanced toward the door, and her heartbeat stuttered. She couldn't have pictured Chris more handsome. Looking both gorgeous and refined, he sported a black tuxedo and red bow tie. Her breath caught, and for several moments she just stared at him. Their eyes locked. His smile made her blush.

He walked over to her, but to her it seemed he glided, feet never touching the floor.

"You look absolutely stunning." Chris slid his hands around her waist.

She blushed. "You look quite handsome yourself, Mr. Chandler."

His kiss was soft. The taste of him lingered on her lips, leaving a longing behind.

"I brought company," he said, turning slightly toward the entrance.

Serenity looked past Chris to see his entire family checking in at the table her mother manned. Kent, Ray and Brynn, accompanied by a woman she didn't recognize, were also there.

"Thank you!" Serenity wrapped her arms around him and planted a kiss right on his lips.

Together they walked over to greet Mr. and Mrs. Chandler and their daughters. From the mother to the youngest sister, the Chandler women looked stunning. Chris introduced his family and friends to Serenity's parents. The other woman was Kent's new girlfriend, Marita.

"This is lovely, Serenity. We'll have to talk about having your gala at Chandler's next year, dear." Mrs. Chandler nodded.

"I'd love that, Mrs. Chandler."

Mr. Chandler gently placed his hand on the small of his wife's back. "No business tonight, honey. Let's enjoy ourselves."

"I was just saying…" Mrs. Chandler's voice trailed off as Mr. Chandler guided her toward the bar.

Serenity shook her head and chuckled. Just as she was about to walk away, she saw a familiar figure in the corner of her eye. With a double take, she recognized Storm Kensington and looked at Chris.

Chris shrugged. "I reminded him about it and he wanted to come."

"Oh! The kids are going to lose it!" Serenity was delighted.

She greeted Storm, introduced him to Rayne, Elisa and her parents, and refused to allow him to purchase a ticket.

Chris's family mingled with the crowd. Soon the cocktail hour was over, and dinner was served while the band played more upbeat songs. The program officially began with Rayne and Serenity welcoming their guests and playing a video featuring kids from the program, several of whom credited the program and learning to play instruments with keeping them off the streets and out of trouble. The mission was clear—Heartstrings helped kids build confidence, learn skills and discover talents as an alternative to the streets.

After that, the kids performed. When they finished their first number, two of them left their instruments behind and ran over to Storm. Willingly, he joined them on the stage and played the next song with them. Serenity hadn't realized he'd brought his violin in with him. When their piece was done, Storm graced them with a solo that mesmerized the entire crowd. Serenity was in tears by the time he was done. She couldn't believe this was happening. To finish, he played one more upbeat number, bringing the crowd to their feet.

Next, they honored a local music teacher and an artist, both of whom spent considerable time giving back to their communities. One of their most-improved students took the podium and shared his personal journey of how Heartstrings had helped him discover a talent that he'd never realized he had and that saved him from joining a gang. His new passion had taken him away from a bad crowd and had changed his life. Immediately after his moving story, Rayne and Serenity appealed to the crowd, who offered pledges and donations to help the organization continue their mission.

Storm stood, pulling a check from the inner pocket of his tuxedo jacket, and presented it to Rayne and Serenity. Their eyes bulged when they saw that he'd donated fifty thousand dollars, which was by far the largest donation they'd received to date. Serenity fought back tears. Mr. Chandler followed suit with another fifty thousand–dollar donation from his family. Serenity's knees weakened. She didn't think she'd be able to stand through the remainder of the program, but she managed.

"On behalf of the youth we serve through Heartstrings every week, we thank you." Rayne presented closing remarks. "Now let's dance!" She shimmied away from the podium right into Ethan's arms.

The band played louder. The lead singer took the microphone and belted out an old party-starting song, bringing everyone to the floor. Serenity found her way through the crowd of dancers and landed in Chris's arms.

"You did an amazing job," Chris said.

"This night couldn't have been better." Serenity was giddy. Partly from pride and partly from fatigue.

"Now let's dance." Chris pulled her onto the dance floor next to their parents.

They danced until beads of sweat glistened on Serenity's chest, and the balls of her feet stung in her stilettos.

"Excuse me, miss," Chris teased without missing a step. "Do you have any plans after this?"

"Yes. I'm going to sleep for two days straight." Serenity threw her head back and laughed. Chris kissed her neck.

"Can I join you?" His voice was husky.

"Absolutely, even though I don't think we'll do much sleeping." Her voice had lowered too.

Chris winked and flashed a slick smile. Serenity laughed again, feeling carefree for the moment. They danced until Serenity had to kick off her shoes, and then they danced some more. After a while, guests came to her and Rayne on the floor to say their goodbyes and wish them well.

Exhausted and elated, Serenity and her team cleaned up after the last of the guests had departed. Chris stayed behind to help, and then they headed to his house. When they arrived, he complimented her once again on a successful event, told her how amazing she was and acknowledged how much of an impact she would have on the lives of the young people she worked with. This talk filled Serenity's heart.

Chris continued to compliment her as they made love in his bed, leaving her proud, sated and spent. Holding her in his arms, he began to snore lightly. Relishing the moment, she wondered how many more times they would have together like that. As tired as she was, these thoughts kept sleep at bay.

Things were going so well between them. Her feelings for him deepened daily. Chris had become important to her. His presence was her fresh air. Would all of that fizzle away when she left?

## Chapter 26

Chris woke feeling refreshed. Easing his arms from under Serenity's sleeping body, he carefully climbed out of bed, trying not to wake her. After a quick trip to the bathroom, he stood staring out over the water at the bedroom window. The picturesque view of the lake was the sole reason he had settled on this house. Dawn and dusk were the most breathtaking times for this.

Serenity had been weighing heavily on his mind lately. He turned to watch the rhythmic rise and fall of her bare breasts. She was beautiful even as she slept. Her smooth almond skin looked angelic against the stark-white linens. The sheets, wrapped around her shapely curves, seemed like a setup for the perfect picture. He felt the sudden urge to run his fingers through the fluffy coils of hair sprawled across the pillow. Yet, he still stood, watching her breathe, admiring her splendor.

Since she had entered his life, he hadn't thought of any other woman. She managed to arrest his full focus. No woman had ever successfully done that before, though some had come close. He no longer debated the logic of having to know someone for a certain amount of time before committing yourself. The months felt like years already, but in the best possible way. The fact that he'd met her online no longer made a difference. He'd stopped wondering how she'd managed to have him so smitten in a relatively short period of time. All that mattered was how he felt about her in that very moment and the fact that it felt like love.

Chris had introduced Serenity to his family and received confirmation that she was an amazing catch. They adored her and agreed that she was a perfect fit for him. When she woke, he was going to express what he'd been feeling.

He pulled a fresh pair of boxers from the drawer and stepped into them. He then headed down to his state-of-the-art kitchen to rustle up some kind of breakfast. Without having had much time to shop, he found the refrigerator didn't yield much. He had two eggs, a pat of butter and one last slice of bread left—the undesired end of the loaf. Closing the fridge, he trotted up the steps to his room. Breakfast in bed would have to happen another time. If they wanted to eat, they were going to have to leave the house.

"Serenity." He called her name softly, giving a gentle shake to her shoulder.

He nudged her two more times before she responded. Her eyes fluttered. She groaned.

"Morning." Chris admired her as she blinked against the light pouring in through the large windows.

"Hey." Her voice was hoarse.

"Hungry?"

Serenity nodded and stretched, extending her limbs in opposite directions.

"Let's get dressed." Chris slid his arms under Serenity's legs and back and lifted her up. She giggled.

With the sheet dangling below, Chris carried her to the adjoining bathroom. He placed her upright, steadily on her feet and started several heads in the walk-in shower. Water sprayed from the top and pulsated from the sides. They bathed one another, creating more steam than the hot water could be credited for.

Within the hour, they were seated at a quaint eatery—one of the few besides the traditional diners that opened early enough for breakfast. In the car, Chris had mentioned that the place was family owned and operated. Serenity gushed about the cozy feel, accomplished with antique furnishings being grouped into unique seating arrangements. The mature woman who greeted Chris with a warm, matronly hug sat them at a beautiful, distressed table flanked by two plush wing chairs.

Serenity looked around. "So much of this place reminds me of my grandmother's house. It feels like someone's living room."

"And the food is amazing."

"I can't wait to taste it." Serenity looked up at the waitress handing her the menu. "Thanks." She smiled. The waitress nodded and left. "What do you suggest?" she asked Chris, opening the menu.

"Almost everything is delicious. I usually get the poached eggs with the crab cake, or the asparagus and lump crab omelet."

"Goodness! There's such a thing? My mouth is watering already. Where's that on the menu?"

Chris pointed. "Right here, and you'll be happy to know that everything is organic and grass-fed."

The waitress came back and took their orders.

"Tell me the truth. How did everything go last night?" Serenity cringed as if she were waiting for Chris to spew a bad report.

"I told you last night that you and your team did an awesome job."

"I know. Thanks. I get crazy about these events." A sense of relief was apparent in her exhalation. "Thanks to your family and Storm, we raised more than we ever have. I have to do something to show your family my appreciation."

"No need. We're huge humanitarians. When we see worthy causes, we do what we can to support them. That's why we started the foundation."

Serenity smiled, but it quickly disappeared. Chris could sense that something was wrong but couldn't imagine what would chase her smile away so suddenly.

"Are you all right?" he asked.

Averting her eyes, she sighed and pressed her lips together. His chest knotted. He'd come to acknowledge his true feelings for her, and now it looked as though she was about to hit him with bad news. She remained quiet for several moments. Her eyes were fixed on the table. He knew she was searching for the right words. His stomach knotted along with his chest.

"What is it?" His voice elevated. He couldn't take the silence. "What's wrong?"

"It's good and bad news."

"Give me the bad news first." Chris braced himself.

"I have to leave."

"Leave what? Who?" *This isn't happening.* "What are you talking about, Serenity?"

"The grant proposal that I submitted for the work in that remote village of Brazil was approved for funding... by your family's foundation."

"Yes. Of course. I knew that. Remember?" Chris couldn't tell for sure if Serenity was smiling or frowning. The result was a mix of both.

"I know." She released a slow sigh. "Now that the program has been funded, I'm the one who has to go to Brazil to run it."

"What's bad about that?" He knit his brow. "That's great news! When will you have to leave?"

"In a few weeks, once school lets out. I'll have to be there for about a year. I can come home in December but will have to go back around February."

Chris sat back. He took a slow, deep breath. "I see."

For several moments, neither of them spoke.

"I don't know what to do, Chris."

Chris thought carefully before speaking. He quickly determined that the mention of her leaving didn't change how he felt at all. He also decided that he wasn't about to give up easily on what they had.

Chris took her hands in his. "Serenity." He looked directly into her eyes. "This doesn't change how I feel about you at all. I want you whether you're here on Long Island or thousands of miles away across the globe. We can work this out. You can come home for holidays and long weekends, or I can go there."

"That's the problem, Chris. I can't afford to travel back and forth so much, and the budget that was submitted in the grant is pretty lean. The most I could come home each semester is once—maybe twice?"

The forlorn look on her face pierced his soul.

"Then I'll come to you, as much as possible. I'm not going to let you get away."

Serenity's smile pushed through her frown. "You mean that?"

"Definitely. I need you to understand that you mean a lot to me. I've been wrestling with how I've been feeling about you for a while now. You're an incredible woman. I want to be with you. Geography doesn't change that."

"I've never been in a long-distance relationship before." Serenity didn't sound hopeful.

"Neither have I, but I'm confident we can work through this. It's only a year."

Pouting, she tilted her head and regarded him with a doe-eyed look. "You really think so, Chris?"

"All I know is, I don't want to let you go."

"I don't want to let you go, either."

Chris stood and pulled Serenity up with him. Squeezing her in his embrace, he whispered in her ear. "I think you've definitely put something on me. I've never fallen for anyone so hard and so fast in my life."

She giggled. "I guess we're even then because I've been questioning myself about how fast I've fallen for you too."

Chris held her face in his hands and kissed her lips. The moment they sat back down, their food arrived.

"When you finalize your dates, we'll schedule my visits, but we can talk about that later. Right now my stomach is growling."

When Serenity smiled, a spark flashed in her eyes. Something inside of Chris shifted, and he felt his desire for her grow even more. His new goal was to keep that spark shining, and he was willing to do whatever was necessary. He wasn't happy about the idea of not seeing her whenever he felt the need to touch her supple skin, but there was no way he was going to release the one woman who had truly captured his heart.

# Chapter 27

Serenity thought back to her last night with Chris before leaving for Brazil. He had made love to her so sweetly that tears had rolled down her cheeks. If she wasn't mistaken, he may have shed a few too. She wasn't sure. Now as she arranged the clothes in the closet in her room, she marveled at how quickly the weeks had breezed by. The pace had been frenzied, between Rayne's bridal shower, the wedding, Serenity's trip preparations, and the surprise going-away party, hosted by Rayne, Elisa and Chris at Chandler's. Serenity chuckled, remembering how those bittersweet tears seemed unstoppable and how she'd made everyone else cry. She shook her head and returned to the present.

The night was still fairly young, but the sky was already midnight blue. Crowds of stars sprinkled against the velvety backdrop. She longed for Chris—to hear him whisper in her ear or hold her head in his hands and kiss her lips. She'd called from the airport the day before to let him know she had arrived safely in Brazil and had tried to no avail to connect several times since then. The signal near the village was too weak for them to carry on a tolerable conversation using her current carrier. If the call connected at all, she'd hear a solid silence or pieces of every other word. She also hadn't spoken to her parents or friends since shortly after her arrival. The failed communication expanded the distance between them all. Serenity didn't know how she would survive without being able to hear Chris's voice. She'd fallen asleep in his arms every single night in the weeks leading up to her departure. The first night's sleep had been facilitated by travel fatigue. She wasn't sure about the nights that would follow, including tonight.

Darcy had promised to take her the following day to his neighborhood or to the city, where the signals were stronger. She planned to buy one of those prepaid phones from a local provider to see if that would allow her to communicate with folks back home. By then, she would have gone more than a full day without speaking to Chris. She wondered if he missed her as terribly as she missed him.

Even though she had worked with Darcy for years before his return to Brazil, she still felt incredibly alone.

It was too early to sleep. The host family she was staying with buzzed around in the kitchen in anticipation of the great-smelling dinner the woman of the house was cooking up. Serenity smiled as she passed them on her way out to the porch and sat in one of the wooden chairs with seats made of straw. A single light provided just enough illumination for her to feel safe. She looked down the stone path leading up to the door. Bushy flora shone in the moonlight. The quiet was as thick as the night, save for the unfamiliar sounds of insects or whatever those animals were that screeched in the distance. She stayed outside but scooted closer to the door. The air held a freshness that didn't exist in New York. Taking a deep breath, she let it out slowly and smiled. This was going to be an amazing experience, she reminded herself.

Serenity had chosen the option of staying with a host family rather than in a hotel. Their warm, single-level home was closer to the village and would allow her to immerse herself in the culture. The furnishings were simple, with wooden tables that looked to have been carved right out of the trees. Knitted throws in bright colors covered beds, chairs and couches, making the three-bedroom house cozy.

She reminisced on her short time in Salvador de Bahia. She was still in awe of the varying landscape they covered on their way to the school. She had sat wide-eyed, absorbing the changing scenery, finding both sadness and beauty in all of it. Contemporary urban skylines and exquisite homes stood juxtaposed to the harsh reality of the impoverished shantytowns a short distance away. Tiny, stacked homes lay slanted against lush rolling hills or a stone's throw from the vast blue ocean. When Serenity exited the car in the village, she had felt drawn to touch the red soil under her feet. Sporadic, lush greenery sprouted from that soil. Small dwellings bore vibrant hues.

Meeting the kids had been the highlight. She'd fallen in love with them immediately. They hugged her, held her hand, and skipped while Darcy gave her a tour of the flat, plain school building. She couldn't wait to begin working with them.

A while later, the father came home, and Serenity joined the family for a dinner of chicken, fish stew and rice. Lucas and Isabelle were an older couple who spoke a level of broken English that enabled her to communicate about the basics with them. Their young, adult daughter,

Ana, was relatively fluent and would help her parents out when they struggled with English.

"I desperately want to visit America," Ana said over a forkful of rice. "I've been thinking about attending my next level of university there." She then spoke in her native tongue. Serenity assumed Ana was translating her own words when the mother smiled proudly and the father nodded.

"What part?"

"New York, of course."

"Be sure to let me know. I'll show you around."

"That would be wonderful. You can help me perfect my English, and I will help you with your Portuguese."

"I hope I'm not mangling your language too much." Serenity laughed. In preparation for her trip, she had taken lessons and practiced with a few language apps. She wanted to sound as authentic as possible but knew her American accent stood in the way. "You can certainly help me do a better job."

"You're doing very well. Believe me, I've heard some really bad Portuguese in my time, and I'm sure my English could be better. I'll perfect it when I come to America to stay for a while."

"That always helps."

Through the rest of dinner, Serenity learned more about the family she was staying with. Lucas was a carpenter and sold distinctive pieces to rich families, and Isabelle was a volunteer with the school in the village, when she wasn't making clothes. They'd put their talents to good use and enjoyed a comfortable living. Ana was finishing up college and preparing for the grad level.

After dinner, Serenity retreated to her room to retire early. Between the kids, food and hospitality, she was sure she was going to enjoy her stay. The only thing missing was Chris.

She tried to reach him one more time before going to bed but couldn't maintain a fair enough signal. She closed her eyes and imagined his voice, wishing he were there to whisper in her ear and hold her until she fell asleep, the way he did every time they spent the night together. She closed her eyes with a smile on her lips. Sure enough, he showed up in her dreams. They lay, indulging in each other's presence, on a beautiful beach. When she woke the next morning, Serenity was upset that Chris was gone.

She was all ready to go when Darcy arrived. "Ready?" He spoke English with the influence of his native tongue. The cadence was musical to her. When they had worked together in New York, he hadn't seemed to have an accent at all.

"I'm ready! I need to get one of those phones we talked about."

"Yeah. It should help some. Service can still be bad in the village at times, but it should be much better than the service from your regular phone. Let's go. We've got some sightseeing to do. Once we start at school, you'll have less time to hang out like this."

"I'm in!"

Their first stop was a store where she could buy a phone. Immediately, she called Chris. She nearly screamed when he answered.

"Chris! Babe! Can you hear me?"

"Babe, I can hear you fine. I almost didn't answer because the number was weird."

"Ah!" Serenity laughed, tickled by her own excitement. "I know. I got a phone from a local provider. I'm so glad to hear your voice. What time is it there?"

"Just after eleven in the morning. What time is it there?"

"Around noon." Serenity filled him in on every moment since their last conversation. "I can't wait to see you. I feel like three more weeks is going to be way too long. I hope this phone works well when I get back to the house."

"I hope so too. It's been too long since I heard your voice."

"Actually, it's only been two days." She laughed, realizing it really hadn't been that long. It just felt longer.

"Two days too long without hearing from you."

They talked for a few more minutes before Serenity reluctantly said goodbye. She blushed at the sound of Chris sending her a kiss through the phone. Serenity called her parents and girlfriends next and promised to stay in touch as much as possible. After spending the day seeing much of what Salvador had to offer, Darcy and Serenity made their way back to the house. She tried Chris again once she got there. As Darcy had mentioned, the signal was stronger but wasn't always guaranteed. Serenity had a brief, choppy conversation with Chris for a few moments before heading to bed. Fortunately, she dreamed of him.

## Chapter 28

Chris had been optimistic when Serenity had first told him about her trip. Sure that the distance wouldn't impact their relationship, he had assured her that they could work it out. Chris expected to have visited her by now, but work had thrown a major glitch in his plans. Now they struggled through two weeks of sporadic communication. The distance between them affected him more that he'd anticipated. He had known he would miss her, but the void gaped wider than he'd expected and touched him deeper than he'd thought possible.

Dialing her new number, he was prepared to count the rings until she picked up. The call went straight to voice mail. At least he could hear her recorded voice. He didn't bother leaving a message. He knew it was likely that she was inside one of the school buildings. Instead, he sent a text.

Thinking about you.

Chris huffed, put the phone on his desk and sat back. He craved her with every part of him. His fingers longed to stroke her hair. His lips desired to graze her hot skin. His arms yearned to wrap themselves around her body. His mind wanted the stimulation she generated. He needed to feel her inside and out. His heart…it ached for all of her.

Chris pulled his chair closer to the desk and tapped on the keyboard, bringing up the travel site he often used. Fingering days on his desk calendar, he entered the dates for the upcoming weekend. A list of prices populated the screen. Chris was searching departure times when his desk phone rang.

"This is Chris."

"Son, come to my office. We need to meet now."

"Be right there, Dad." Chris could tell from the urgency of his father's tone there was something serious going on. Before standing, he looked at the list of flights. He'd find one after meeting with him. While he was in his office, Chris could tell his dad he was taking Thursday and Friday off so he could head to Brazil to satisfy his longing to see Serenity.

"Do you know what this is about?" Jewel asked, catching up with him in the corridor.

"Not yet."

Jewel sighed. "I just hope it's not more bad news. If another chain closes, I'm going to scream. These supermarkets are leaving neighborhoods in droves."

"The gap is widening fast. It's getting harder to fill it. This would be the fourth one this month. That will be a huge chunk of business if we don't get these new owners."

The siblings sighed simultaneously.

Bobby Dale was just hanging up the phone when they walked into his office. His assistant, Emily, and Greg, a man from accounting, were already there. Jewel and Chris sat on either side of their father's desk.

"Hey!" His father scooted closer to his desk and picked up a pen and notepad. Scribbling a quick memo, he handed it to Jewel.

Jewel skimmed the note. "Friday!" She looked up in shock.

"We have to work fast."

"What's Friday?" Chris asked. Emily and Greg's expressions also reflected inquiry.

Jewel looked at Chris.

"You and Jewel will meet with the owners of Organic Haven, a boutique supermarket chain. They're opening forty-five locations across the tri-state area. We've managed to get on their calendar for this Friday. I'll need the two of you to fly up on Thursday night to meet with them the next day and come home with some business. This is almost a sure thing. I have the CEO roundtables and can't make it myself, so, Chris, I'll need you to guarantee that you can close this deal." His father turned to Greg, pointing his pen in his direction. "Greg. I'll need you to run the numbers. I want an update on the impact of the closings on our budget for this quarter and forecasts for the next quarter."

Chris's heart sank. Duty called at the most inopportune time. He wanted to see Serenity this weekend. No. He needed to see Serenity. There was no way to get out of this. Jewel ran operations and, besides his father, Chris was the company's best closer. They needed this contract. Chris took a deep breath and let it out slowly. Kent and Ray would have to handle The Reserve on their own too.

Just before his father had called him for this meeting, he had been looking forward to telling Serenity that he was coming to see her. Now he had to wait at least another week.

Bringing his attention back to the people in the room,

he strategized with the team about their approach and getting the final numbers for how much of a financial gap they were dealing with. By the time they were done, Emily had their flight scheduled. They agreed to meet again before he and Jewel left to finalize their proposal for the supermarket chain.

Chris maintained a professional demeanor through the entire meeting. In his office, he closed the door, leaned against it and groaned. Rolling the kinks that tightened the muscles in his neck, he walked over to his desk and flopped into the seat. Minutes passed before he moved. Would their relationship survive much longer without communication? He had to think about that. Not seeing her didn't make him care for Serenity any less. Instead, her absence reverberated in the hollows of his chest. Missing her had become physical. It surprised him. In the past, absence helped him forget. He moved on seamlessly. Not this time. He couldn't see moving forward without Serenity. He had to find a way to make this work.

He picked up his phone, pulled up her name and stared at the foreign number listed below her usual cell number in his contact list. He wanted to hear her voice. He tapped the screen and put the phone to his ear.

"Chris!" Serenity's excitement made his pulse beat faster.

He sat up. "Serenity?" he questioned as if it could have been someone else.

"Hi. Can you hear me?"

"Yes." Her voice was choppy, but he could still make out what she was saying.

"You called at a perfect time. We're headed into a town near the village. My signal should be—"

Serenity's voice was cut off midsentence.

"Hello?…Serenity?"

"Chr...I...you...hear me?"

"No. You're coming in and out." He figured out what she was saying.

"When are you coming?" She sounded sweet.

Chris heard that and air swirled in his chest. His shoulders slumped. He wished he could tell her that he'd see her this week. He'd already postponed once already because of issues at work.

"I'm trying to come next week."

"Next week?" Despite the spotty connection, her disappointment rang through with crisp clarity.

Chris pictured her posture slump as a frown crossed her pretty lips, and he wished he could wrap his arms around her.

"You changed your plans again?"

"Yes. I'm sorry."

Then there was silence.

He wasn't sure if it was the connection or if she just didn't have anything else to say to him.

"I'm coming to you soon. I promise... Hello?"

"Hel..."

"Serenity?"

No response. A series of beeps indicated that the call had ended. He tried her number again. The call went to voice mail. He tried again, only to have the same result. He wouldn't be able to explain anyway.

Chris put the phone down, rested his elbows on his desk and held his head in his hands. One way or another, he was going to find his way to Serenity. He had to.

## Chapter 29

After nearly a month, the students were already playing well. The sounds coming from the instruments began to sound more like music. Serenity walked into the main room where most of the learning took place, and several students ran over to her to hug her waist. With a heart filled with warmth, Serenity hugged them back.

"Okay, everyone. Get your instruments." When it was time to play, their eyes would brighten, some would literally jump up and down. Wood grunted against the stone floor as students knocked into each other in pursuit of their respective instruments lining the back wall. Their excitement filled her with overwhelming joy.

Serenity looked forward like never before to teaching. The only sore spot in her life was her dwindling relationship with Chris. Despite her new phone, they hardly spoke. The signals just weren't strong enough in the village or at the house. She only got to the city once, maybe twice, a week. Almost every conversation was a struggle. She was beginning to think that trying to hold on to him during this trip was a mistake.

She wanted to be upset at him for postponing his visit

twice already but couldn't really blame him. At times, her imagination would get the best of her, and she'd entertain the idea that he was probably ready to move on. Finding another woman to spend time with wasn't hard for a man who was handsome, rich and charming. Then she'd scold herself for jumping to conclusions that caused such sadness.

"Ms. Serenity." She felt a hand tug on her dress. "We're ready." The small, heavily accented voice brought her back to the present.

"Yes. Thank you." She patted the boy on the shoulder.

For the remainder of her classes, Serenity forced herself to stay focused on her students. Thinking about Chris only made her feel worse. When the day was over, she saw that he'd tried to call. As much as she missed him, she went to bed without trying to call him back. She needed time with her thoughts before speaking to him again.

She woke with a renewed perspective. The obstacles weren't his fault. She would try to stay positive and not assume anything. He had said he'd make it work, and she wanted to give him a chance to do just that before giving up on what they'd created. Her renewed spirit had her looking forward to speaking to Chris again—and seeing him soon.

"Good morning…" Serenity called Chris before she'd gotten out of bed. "I said *good morning*. Can you hear me?"

"Barely." His reply was chopped by dense silence.

"Hold on." Serenity slid her foot into the slippers beside her bed and tiptoed through the house. Carefully, she pushed the front door open, trying to keep the creak from waking anyone. "Can you hear me better?" she yelled into the phone, after closing the door behind her.

She moved around on the porch, hoping to find a spot that provided more clarity.

"I can…" Chris's voice faded and came back in.

Serenity moved all the way to the edge of the porch. Finally, she could hear him more steadily.

"Say that again."

"I said *how are you*?" Chris yelled into the phone.

"Oh. Great! Missing you," Serenity yelled back. The two maintained high volumes throughout the call.

"I don't have good news."

Serenity felt her pulse pause. "What's wrong? Is everything okay? Did something happen?"

"I'm going to have to push my trip back another week. We have new client meetings, and they're critical for business. I tried to work out other dates, but this seems to be the only one that worked for everyone else."

Serenity's heart fell to the pit of her stomach. She blinked back tears. Surprised at her own reaction, she shook her head and pulled herself together. "Oh," was all she could manage to say. As much as she wanted to see Chris, she truly needed a taste of familiarity. She loved her work and adored the people she worked with—especially the kids. She had begun to fall in love with the city but was still terribly homesick. His visit would have been her salve, soothing more than just her desire for home.

"Serenity."

After a moment she finally replied. "I'm here."

"Babe. I'm really sorry."

"Sure."

"Are you okay? It's just another week. I don't foresee any other issues."

"Yes…yes. I'm fine." Truthfully, she was crestfallen. She could feel the slump in her posture.

Again Chris was pushing back the dates of his visit. At first he was coming two weeks after her arrival. Then it was four weeks. Now it was changing again. Serenity couldn't handle the frustration of anticipating his presence and having that excitement doused by constant postponements. In the weeks that she'd been away, she'd hardly spoken to him as it was. Maybe trying to continue their relationship was too much to ask. Perhaps she should concentrate on her work and, when she returned to the states for good, they could try to rebuild what they had started—if there was anything to salvage.

"Are you there?" Chris's voice broke into her thoughts.

"Yes…I'm here." Serenity sat in the wood-and-straw chair. The signal faded. Not bothering to call back, she thought that maybe parting would be best.

She looked down at her phone. It hadn't rung, which meant that he hadn't called back or he couldn't get through. Either way, she decided to let the relationship fade like their troubled connections. She wouldn't force it. At some point in the future, it wouldn't hurt as much.

## Chapter 30

A week had passed without a word from Serenity. Nor had she responded to texts or email. Chris wasn't even sure if she was receiving any of his messages. He wondered if something had happened to her. Worry set in, and horrible imagined scenarios became viable possibilities. After the third day of worrying, he showed up at her parents' home. Surprised by his visit, they invited him in and offered him dinner.

Chris tried not to alarm them. Instead, he spoke as if all were well, trying to gauge if they knew anything that he didn't. They hadn't acted as if there were an issue.

"Trying to get Serenity on the phone can be a chore sometimes."

"I know!" her mother said. "I was finally able to have a decent conversation with her yesterday. She'd taken a trip into the city, and our entire conversation was clear. I wish it could be like that all the time."

Mrs. Williams's comment put him at ease. At least he knew that Serenity was alive, but why hadn't she called him while she was in the city? They could have spoken then. He thought about the other reason he needed to see her parents and paused to talk with them a little longer before heading for the door.

Mr. Williams patted his back. "See you soon, son," he said as Chris trotted down the porch steps.

Two days later, Chris still hadn't heard from Serenity, and she still wasn't responding to emails or texts. He couldn't be certain she had received any of his attempts at reaching her but, if she had, why wasn't she responding?

Their lack of communication created a void so deep, Chris thought it would consume him. A piece of him seemed to have been hijacked. Serenity's absence was profound and resonated in several areas of his life. Even his home seemed emptier without her around. It was one thing not to be able to see her face, but not being able to at least hear her voice made him realize that his feelings for her were more than he had anticipated.

Before she had left, he'd told her that she meant a lot to him, but that was putting it lightly. Chris now realized he loved her. Her absence had confirmed it. He was determined to do something about it. Sitting back in his office chair, he squeezed his eyes shut. What could he do?

Chris jumped up from his chair and headed to his father's office.

"Dad!" He pushed his way in without checking to see if anyone else was in there. Chris marched to his father's desk as he was ending a call. "I need a few days."

"What's going on, son? Did something happen?"

"I'm not sure." Chris paced the floor in front of his father's desk.

"Is it Serenity?"

"Yes."

Alarm registered across his father's face and he stood to his feet. "What do we need to do?"

"I'm not sure yet. I need to go down there and find out. I haven't heard from her in days."

"Do you need me to come with you?"

"Thanks, Dad." Chris was relieved that his father was willing to go. "I'm sure I can handle it. I'll call you when I know more."

"I can get you a charter."

"That would be perfect."

Bobby Dale was already dialing by the time Chris finished speaking. "What time do you want to leave?"

"Late tonight."

"Done!" his father said. "We will handle things here."

Chris left his dad's office feeling empowered. He was getting closer to Serenity and whatever issue kept her from getting back to him. Since his father was arranging a private flight, he could have left that afternoon, but he had a few things to do before boarding. Tonight would be soon enough. He remembered Serenity giving him a number to contact her in Salvador de Bahia in case of an emergency. He tried to remember the name. Finally, it came to him. Searching his phone, Chris called Darcy that night before going to bed. He confirmed that Serenity was okay but expressed that she seemed to be having a hard time adjusting to the move at times. Chris asked him not to tell her about his call so he could surprise her.

Despite being happy that nothing terrible had happened to her, he was annoyed by the fact that she hadn't contacted him.

Chris left New York on Thursday night. Nearly fourteen hours later, he arrived at the airport in Salvador, Brazil. His driver, provided by Darcy, met him at the airport. Chris went to his hotel in the middle of the city before heading to the village. He made the last of his arrangements from there.

He hadn't bothered trying to call Serenity again so that he wouldn't spoil the surprise. He was tired but refused to give in to the travel fatigue threatening to slow him down. By the time he reached Darcy's house, school would be over. The plan was for Darcy to lead the way to where Serenity was staying, with Chris's car following his. It was a Friday. She wouldn't be expected back at school until Monday. That was more than enough time for Chris to get what he needed from her.

Fatigue got the better of him, and he couldn't help but fall asleep on the long ride to Darcy's house. Darcy got in his car and led the way to Serenity's billet. After twenty minutes, Darcy pulled off the dirt road and stopped in front of a modest ranch house. She was sitting on the porch under the evening sun with a younger woman. She stood when she saw Darcy's car but paused when she spotted the other car behind it.

From inside the vehicle, Chris could see her squinting to see who it was. Being only yards away made his pulse thump faster. The sight of her face gave him pause. Six weeks had passed since she'd left, but the void her departure had created had made it feel like several months. She'd taken his breath away with her. Seeing her face made him breathe more easily.

Serenity started toward the first car and stopped abruptly when Chris stepped out of his. Her eyes widened and her hands flew to her mouth. Standing frozen, she stared as if she were assessing whether or not he was real. She remained stuck on the spot until he had made his way over to her.

The young woman called Serenity's name, but she didn't answer. Darcy stood by. Everyone seemed to wait for her to respond.

"Serenity." Her name felt good on his lips. Chris touched her face.

Serenity blinked, and tears spilled from her eyes.

"What happened?" Chris asked, needing to understand her answer.

"I…what are you doing here?"

"I didn't hear from you. I got worried but, when I went to your parents' and they told me they had spoken to you, I got mad. I'm here for answers."

"You came all the way to Brazil for an answer?"

"I came for you."

Serenity's mouth opened and closed, but no words passed through.

"Now tell me what happened."

"I…" Serenity sighed, cast her eyes downward and shook her head. "I figured you didn't want this anymore. I…was weaning myself from you so the absence wouldn't hurt so much."

Chris looked confused. "Why?"

Serenity let her hands fall by her sides with a slap. She shook her head again. "When you kept postponing the trip, I thought I was losing you. It was hard not seeing you, not hearing from you."

"Come with me." Chris took her hand.

"Where are we going?" Serenity looked from Chris to Darcy to the young woman. Darcy's only response was a smile.

"Just get your purse. I have something special for you."

"Okay." Serenity ran inside and returned moments later with a small handbag.

"Thank you, Darcy." Chris turned to Ana and extended his hand.

"Hello. I'm Ana." Her English was near perfect.

"It's nice to meet you, Ana. Don't worry. I'll bring her back safely."

Ana giggled and then nodded. "Okay."

Chris took Serenity by the hand and started toward the car. Stopping halfway, he turned, cupped her cheeks in his hands and kissed her. The taste of her lips almost overwhelmed him. Chris forced himself to pull away.

"I'm sorry." Serenity's voice was a whisper.

Chris took her hand once again and led her to the waiting car.

Back at his hotel, words weren't necessary. Chris held her close, staring at her beautiful face as if he were trying to forge a permanent imprint in his mind. He touched her skin to make sure she was real. She did the same to him.

They kissed a trail from the door to the bedroom. He laid her down. Piece by piece, he removed each article of clothing, planting soft kisses on every part that lay bare. Serenity removed his garments with the same care. He reacquainted himself with her body, handling her with care and unmistakable admiration. His erection was like stone. He wanted her but preferred to savor their encounter. He needed to take his time.

He kissed her lips again. She wrapped her arms around his naked body. Their kisses deepened as they drank each other in. Coerced by his insatiable craving, he caressed every inch of her body until her skin grew warm under his touch. He nibbled her ears and nipples, before sinking between her thighs. He captured her bud between his lips. Serenity gasped and cried out. Grabbing his head from behind, she pushed him deeper. Chris lapped at her until her cries turned into pleas, and she scampered away. He watched longingly as spasms ripped through her one after the other. With eyes squeezed tight, her back arched and she panted, groaned and licked her lips. Her body eased flat on the bed as her climax released its hold on her.

Serenity reached for him. Taking his erection into her hand, she tasted him and lapped until he hissed. She covered him with her mouth and milked him between her jaws. He pulled away to keep from reaching his peak too soon. Laying her on her back, he stared into her eyes and entered her. The delicious sensation of her cushioning walls caused his eyes to roll back. He looked back at her. Both refused to look away this time as he drove sweet long strokes inside of her.

"Serenity." He whispered her name.

"Chris." She called him too.

"I love you."

Her initial response was tears rolling down the sides of her face.

"Did you hear me? I love you."

"I love you too, Chris."

At her declaration, his core tightened. Without breaking his stride, he leaned forward and covered her mouth with his. They held each other tighter. It felt like Serenity would never let him go. Chris felt an intense sensation rush to his erection. He moved in and out of her faster, the friction crippling momentarily. He pushed beyond the pleasure threatening to render him immobile. She bucked against him, meeting him halfway. He completely lost control. His rhythmic thrusts became urgent, accompanied by guttural grunts.

"Chris!" Serenity cried out.

A hard, paralyzing release barreled through him. Chris pushed into her as far as he could go. She suctioned him inside her moist walls. He moaned loudly and collapsed on top of her.

When he caught his breath, he rolled over and took her in his arms.

"Promise me you'll never pull away from me again," he said.

"I promise."

He kissed her one more time before falling asleep.

The next morning, they enjoyed room service in bed. Chris told Serenity to hurry so that he could carry out the rest of his plans. They flew by private jet to Rio de Janeiro, where they checked into one of the area's most luxurious hotels. Chris spent the day spoiling Serenity with spa treatments, a lunch filled with indigenous delicacies, and stolen kisses, then they made it to the beach in time to enjoy dusk.

"You've been working tirelessly for months. You deserve to be pampered. Let someone do something for you for a change," he told her.

At first she scolded him for making such a fuss over her, but he ignored her.

Chris purchased a light jacket for Serenity to shield against the cool evening air blowing along the beach. The breeze didn't detract from the beauty of the sparkling blue water. Nature offered a breathtaking show of the sun's descent. Yellow and orange hues illuminated the lower portion of the sky, lighting the ripples in the sea.

They walked hand in hand along the shore. He had other plans but couldn't let this moment pass. The vibrant glow of the evening sun was far too perfect a backdrop.

"Serenity." Chris stopped walking. He'd dropped to one knee by the time she turned around.

"Oh my goodness, Chris!" Serenity covered her mouth.

"I planned to do this later at dinner, but this moment feels right."

"Chris." She gasped his name. Tears rolled down her cheeks.

"Be my wife."

"Yes! Yes! I'll be your wife."

Chris stood, and Serenity leaped into his arms. Holding tight, he spun her around, let her down and kissed the woman who had come to him through the internet and stolen his heart.

"Let's go back to the room so I can put your ring on your finger and make this official."

Serenity threw her head back and laughed. "Let's go."

When they opened the hotel suite's door, a stunning black cocktail dress hung from a rack, and a diamond necklace lay on a table in the center of the room. Serenity walked over to the dress and jewelry and looked it over.

"This is absolutely beautiful."

"Wait right here." Chris ran into the bedroom and emerged minutes later in a tux. "Put your dress on."

"Now?"

"Yes. Please."

"Okay." Serenity sighed but obliged.

Chris disappeared one more time while she slipped into the strapless number that fit perfectly. When he returned, he placed the necklace on her and pointed to shoes in a box at the bottom of the rack.

"You bought shoes too? You're too much."

"You deserve it all."

Once Serenity was dressed, Chris led her out to the balcony overlooking the city's skyline.

"Isn't it beautiful." It wasn't really a question.

Chris took a ring from a small velvet box. "Before you left, I told you that you meant a lot to me. I felt something with you that I'd never felt before. Once you left, I realized what it was. Love. I want you to know that I love you, Serenity—like I've never loved another woman. When I didn't hear from you, I panicked. The thought of living without you seemed illogical. I knew then what I had to do. When I visited your parents, your father happily gave me his blessing. Now, Ms. Williams. Tell me once more that you will be my wife."

Serenity looked at the large, sparkling princess-cut diamond ring and gasped with her hand at her heart. "Mr. Chandler, I'd be honored to be your wife."

Chris slid the ring onto her finger, kissed the back of her hand and pulled her to him for one more passionate kiss.

"Now you'll never have to doubt me again." Chris kissed her one more time.

\* \* \* \* \*

*If you enjoyed this tempting story,*
*check out more of Nicki Night's titles:*

*HER CHANCE AT LOVE*
*HIS LOVE LESSON*
*RIDING INTO LOVE*
*IT STARTED IN PARADISE*

*Available now from Harlequin Kimani Romance!*

KIMANI™
ROMANCE

# COMING NEXT MONTH
## Available December 19, 2017

# Get 2 Free Books,
## Plus 2 Free Gifts —
just for trying the
## Reader Service!

*LOVE*
# Harlequin
# romance?

Join our Harlequin community to share your thoughts and connect with other romance readers!

Be the first to find out about promotions, news, and exclusive content!

Sign up for the Harlequin e-newsletter and download a free book from any series at

**www.TryHarlequin.com**

---

**CONNECT WITH US AT:**

Harlequin.com/Community

 Facebook.com/HarlequinBooks

 Twitter.com/HarlequinBooks

 Instagram.com/HarlequinBooks

Pinterest.com/HarlequinBooks

ReaderService.com

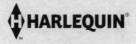

**ROMANCE WHEN
YOU NEED IT**

Want to give in to temptation with
steamy tales of irresistible desire?

Check out **Harlequin® Presents®,
Harlequin® Desire** and
**Harlequin® Kimani™ Romance** books!

## New books available every month!

---

### CONNECT WITH US AT:

Harlequin.com/Community

 Facebook.com/HarlequinBooks

 Twitter.com/HarlequinBooks

 Instagram.com/HarlequinBooks

 Pinterest.com/HarlequinBooks

ReaderService.com

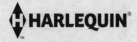

**ROMANCE WHEN
YOU NEED IT**

PGENRE2017